The Explorer of Barkham Street

MARY STOLZ

The *Explorer* of *Barkham Street*

Pictures by
Emily Arnold McCully

A Harper Trophy Book
HARPER & ROW, PUBLISHERS

First Harper Trophy edition, 1987

Library of Congress Cataloging in Publication Data
Stolz, Mary, date
    The explorer of Barkham Street.

    Summary: Reformed bully Martin Hastings fantasizes
about heroic adventures as an explorer and a sports
star, until his new circle of friends and growing self-
confidence at home make real life as exciting as his daydreams.
    1. Children's stories, American. [1. Self-acceptance—
Fiction. 2. Imagination—Fiction. 3. Family life—
Fiction] I. McCully, Emily Arnold, ill. II. Title.
PZ7.S875854Ex 1985   [Fic]   84-48339
ISBN 0-06-025976-0
ISBN 0-06-025977-9 (lib. bdg.)

    (A Harper Trophy Book)
ISBN 0-06-440210-X (pbk.)

To Helen Israel, friend & researcher

The *Explorer* of
Barkham Street

1

Martin Hastings trudged home through the cold early dark, laying plans for the future. Let's see, he said to himself. I'm thirteen now, so in five years I'll be eighteen and Rufus will only be seven. Seven isn't old for a dog, especially a tough mongrel like Rufe.

So.

When he was eighteen he'd go up to that farm where Rufus was now and explain how he and his dog had always planned to be together when the time came, and the time had come so they were going away.

Versions of this scheme had been in his mind for months, and he never got further than the bare announcement. Still, he and Rufus, the two of them, would work it out.

Oh, boy, was it freezing. He clutched his books to his chest for warmth, watching his breath spread on the air before him in white gasps. He fumbled at the ends of his gloves, trying to pull the torn parts over his chilled fingertips. A drop at the end of his nose re-formed each time he leaned over the books to brush it off.

January. Christmas lost forever. Spring, too. Who'd believe in spring on a day like this? No snow, except for what lay like dirty plaster over lawns and the edges of sidewalks.

Berry Madden went by on his bike. Martin waved, but Berry, leaning forward, didn't see him. Probably was afraid to let go of the handlebars. A person could skid on these icy streets. Berry was wearing a ski mask, but even so, Martin didn't see how he could bike on such a day.

"Great weather for penguins," Martin muttered aloud.

The noble emperor penguins of Antarctica faced calmly into the raging, wind-driven blizzard, watching with indifferent eyes as Sir Martin Hastings, sole survivor of Expedition Snowslip ["Swell name!" he congratulated himself] *forged across the pack ice into a force 7 gale, away from the crevasse down which his fellow explorers had just disappeared in a bunch.*

At his back, a hundred-mile-an-hour wind; ahead, frozen wastes; around him, dense and wildly whirling snow. Man-hauling his sled, upon which his faithful lead dog, Rufus, lay exhausted . . .

Martin hunched his shoulders and tried to wrench his mind onto another track. Over a year now since they'd taken his dog from him, that big, wild-hearted puppy he'd named Rufus, and had owned such a short time, but had loved more than anyone or anything else in his life. They'd told him he had to take responsibility for his dog and warned him what they'd do if he didn't and he hadn't and they had, and he still thought it was the unfairest thing that had ever happened to anyone.

He supposed not a day had passed since the afternoon when he came home to find Rufus gone—the empty leash dangling from the backyard run—that he had not thought about his dog. He still had the leash, shoved to the back of his closet. He didn't ache now. Not the way he had at first. And there were plenty of things to keep him busy. Junior high, for one. Lots more homework this year. He was trying, or half trying, to act responsible. In case somebody noticed.

Responsible.

What an awful word. He couldn't even spell it.

5

Ibles and *ables* at the ends of words got away from him. Spelling was hard. And arithmetic. (Arithmetic with an *a* or an *e*?) Anyway, algebra was not arithmetic, it was mathematics, and he couldn't spell that either. He was good at geography. There hadn't been one other person in the class who'd known where Tasmania was in the quiz. Amundsen's company had set out for the South Pole from Tasmania.

Rufus, for the time being, banished to the outposts of his mind, Martin plodded on. His thoughts hung in icicles. He saw himself slung like one of those carcasses in a meat locker, bones and blood exposed, frozen hard as stone, with that fellow, Rocky, punching him for practice. Martin thought in pictures, not in words.

In summer, the colder the water was the better he liked to swim in it, but in winter, on a day like this, the six blocks between home and school seemed more like six miles. The thermometer on the bank building he passed every day had registered two degrees above zero. The explorers of the Poles would've called it a heat wave.

"Some swell explorer you'd have made," Martin snorted.

"Bit young to be talking to yourself, aren't you?" said a man passing by.

6

A year ago, Martin would have yelled something at him. "Practicing up for when I'm an old man like you, Prune Face!" he'd have said. Or something. Now he just ignored the dope.

Twirling and twisting, Martin Hastings, demon center of Barkham Street, sped around the flank of the opposing team. With bulletlike accuracy, he sent the puck spinning and skipping past the menacingly masked goalie, into the net for the WIN! High-fiving all around! Cheers from the crowd! Hugs from his father! Martin, my son, I'm proud of you!

Taking a deep breath, he thought he felt ice crystals forming on his lungs.

"Demon center of Barkham Street," he growled. "Demon dumbbell's more like it."

Oh, but he'd been born in the wrong century. These times were not his times. He should have sailed with Captain Cook; sledged to the polar ice cap with Admiral Peary; gone out to die in the blizzard with brave Lieutenant Oates, to save the lives of his comrades. . . .

Boy, what a laugh. He was even glad he'd lost his paper route, because he'd never have stuck it out through the winter. So there'd have been one more failure to add to the pretty long list of things he'd started and given up on. His bugle. His diet.

8

That awful time he'd tried out for track. What had he ever stuck to, persisted in?

He'd have stuck to anything, persisted in anything, if they'd let him keep his dog. So whose fault was it that no matter what he started, he never reached the finish line?

2

Along Barkham Street, most of the houses had lights
on downstairs, where things were going on, like dinner preparations and conversations about the day,
what everybody had done.

At number 21, where Edward Frost and his family
lived with Edward's dog, Argess, Martin could see
into the living room. Edward was standing there
looking up into his father's face, and Mr. Frost was
looking down with an explaining expression, saying
something.

So? said Martin to himself. So they're having a
conversation. So what?

Just the same, what did they find to talk about,
Edward and his father? They seemed to Martin to
be at it all the time. In summer they'd sit in the
backyard, going on and on, and now a person

couldn't even look in their window without catching the two of them yakking.

Number 23, his own house, had a light upstairs in his sister's room. Downstairs was dark. Depending on the traffic, his father got in between six and seven. His mother, a checker in a downtown market, worked from noon to eight at night. She wasn't home when Martin and Marietta got in from school.

He fumbled with his key, got the door open, then stood in the hall for a moment, shuddering with pleasure at the welcome warmth. He switched on the hall light, walked into the living room and turned on all three lamps, then went into the kitchen and put that light on. He hoped he'd remember to turn some of them off before his father got home.

Martin had asked Marietta one million times to please put on at least a couple of lights when it got dark. Coming home to a lightless house this way was depressing. But, oh no. What Marietta did was go straight to her room, put on her radio, and practice smiling in front of the mirror. Making sure her dimples hadn't disappeared. Or, as this past week, carrying on about a pimple on her chin that you'd think was a pinnacle of human disaster.

Now she came out and stood at the top of the stairs. "That you, Marty?"

11

"No. You think you're seeing Martin Hastings in the skin, but actually you are looking at a clone. A mad scientist in the madness of his insanity has started duplicating me by the thousands."

"He sure *is* crazy. One of you is more than the world needs."

Martin started up, staring at her chin. "Wow— that looks awful. You may have to have your jaw amputated."

"Shut up!"

He started back, arm flung across his brow. "Sister! I was in jest! It's a fine pimple, a pimple of perfection! I have never seen—seen a—"

"Marty. You better leave me alone. I'm warning you."

"It's your night to get dinner started."

"I know that. I was just coming down."

"You know, I've asked you one trillion times to please turn on a couple of lights so people don't have to think they're coming home to the family plot. I mean, you'd think you could do a little thing like turning on—"

"I was too cold to turn on the lights."

Martin gave up. He supposed that made sense to her. "Call this cold?" he said, brushing past her. "The men of Antarctica lived for months in temperatures of fifty to a hundred below. They'd have stripped to the waist on a day like this and sworn by their beards it was a balmy day. Blizzards and force-seven gales meant nothing to them. And I think it's great out. *Cold*, for Admiral Byrd's sake."

"I don't see you stripped to the waist, Admiral. If you ask me, you're full of prunes."

"Full of prunes! How do you *think* of these retorts? I mean, this is a talent you should take before the great American public while we are standing at the crossroads of something."

"Oh, I can't stand it!" Marietta cried out and rushed downstairs, waving her arms over her head. "I can't stand living with you, or anyone in this house! I want to be eighteen years old and away from all of you! Away, away, away . . ."

Martin gaped after her.

What brought that on? They'd been talking to each other this way since he first started to use words, which he was told was when he was only a year old. He'd heard his father say that it had been a tragedy. "They shouldn't be allowed to speak at all until they're at least twelve," his father had said to whoever it had been he was saying it to.

Martin did not, not really, take his father seriously. Everybody had their way of talking, and that was his father's way. Sort of—sarcastic, maybe. A person got used to it. He had supposed that Marietta was used to him, his way of putting things. He didn't mean any harm.

Wondering whether to go down and try to make peace with her, so that when his parents got home they wouldn't dump on him (they just about never dumped on Marietta), he wavered in the hallway, then sighed and went into his room.

It looked okay to him, even though his mother said it might as well be the city dump. Lots of stuff on the floor, of course, but what could you expect when there weren't enough shelves or drawers to put things in? His bugle was sticking out from under the bed. Picking it up, he blew a couple of raw notes, let it fall to the floor. The bugle didn't mean much to him anymore.

There had been a time when he practiced on it by the hour (which had had the additional satisfaction of driving the neighbors crazy). He'd had an idea, back then, that if he got good enough on the bugle, they'd buy him a saxophone. Oh, those crazy sax dreams he'd had, once upon a time!

There was stomping in the aisles and hollering in the streets when Martin Hastings, the world's greatest saxophonist, returned last night to his home-

town after a triumphant world tour. . . .

"Phooey!" said Martin, and kicked the bugle back under his bed.

Opening his closet door, he decided to hang up all the clothes that had fallen off their hangers. That done, he stared around. Sleeping bag on his bed— to save having to make it up every day—all twisted. He straightened it, leaned over, and sniffed. His mother said it smelled.

Coming to a decision, he gathered it up and tramped down to the kitchen.

"Guess I'll just wash this," he said to Marietta, who glanced at him without speaking.

Martin started the wash cycle, tossed in a quantity of detergent.

"You're supposed to measure that," his sister said. "You put in too much."

"Won't hurt, probably. It hasn't been washed in a while."

"It hasn't been washed in a year."

"What's for dinner?"

"Stew."

Mrs. Hastings prepared food in the morning that Marietta and Martin heated at night. There had been a time when she'd made pies and things. Not much of that anymore. Martin didn't see how his mother

15

managed to do as much as she did.

"It seems to me," he said, as he pushed and shoved the sleeping bag into the hot sudsy water, "that we ought to be able to make something like that ourselves. What's to stew? Meat and some potatoes and veg. Any dope could put those together."

"You're calling Mom a dope, you realize."

"Boy, you are *dumb*. I mean, we could help out by—"

"I know what you mean. We couldn't make a stew at this hour in time for dinner."

"I take it back. A person'd have to be smart to act as dumb as you do. What I'm trying to say is, like tonight we could've made a stew, working together—"

"Something we do so well."

"We could give it a whack. And then if we made it one night, the next couple of nights we could eat that, and meanwhile we'd be making something else. I mean, Mom'd flip, wouldn't she?"

"Are you serious?"

"Sure," he said uncertainly. "Anyway, we could try. Once. We could tell Mom to get in some stuff, and then when you got in you could—"

"Oh, *I* could. I see. Well, forget it. What are you going to sleep in tonight? Your undies?"

"Huh?"

"That *thing* you've put in the washer. It isn't going to be dry by the time you go to bed."

"Why not? I'm going to put it in the dryer."

"Brother dear, that is a very cheap sleeping bag. You put it in the dryer and you won't be able to get your feet into it, much less the rest of your"— she looked him up and down—"your bellying body."

Martin turned his head away. *So.* He didn't think they'd noticed that he was pounding toward the poundage again. But leave it to Marietta, he thought dejectedly. He had managed, over the course of the past year, through pluck, grit, and just about starvation, to lose eighteen and a half pounds, but it was coming back. There was a big scale at a drugstore downtown, and if no one was looking, Martin went in there and got on it and quickly off. Of the eighteen and a half he'd lost, he now had nine back.

He looked at his sister angrily. "What am I going to do about my sleeping bag?" he demanded. "Crums, you could've *told* me. What a family! Nobody helps anybody, nobody acts nice to anybody—"

"Stop whining."

Marietta began putting place mats and silverware on the kitchen table. "When the spin cycle is finished, put it on Cool in the dryer to get the damp out, and then hang it in the cellar. I don't know what you'll use tonight. Maybe sheets and blankets like other people?"

With a sense of depression, not helped by the knowledge that his father was due home, Martin walked out of the kitchen.

"What about your great cooking idea?" Marietta called after him. "Shall I tell Mom that we're taking over KP from now on?"

"Ah, shove it in your ear," said her brother, and stamped upstairs. He went in her room, which was forbidden, and turned off her radio. If she complained, he'd say he was too young to have his eardrums punctured.

In his own room, he slammed the door and leaned against it, clenching and unclenching his fists.

What was the darn point to his life? A person came home from school—where if nothing especially bad had happened, nothing good had either—through cold streets to a dark house and a sister who acted as if she couldn't stand him.

Now she was poking fun at his weight. It depressed him to be putting it on again, but the old pluck and grit seemed used up, and he didn't seem to care about things the way a person probably ought to. He didn't care if he got a saxophone. He didn't care if he got another job. He'd had one, delivering news-papers. Got it all on his own. Two weeks later the newspaper people switched to grown-up deliverers with cars. Even if they hadn't, he'd have lost that job. No way he'd have got up on these freezing morn-ings to pedal through dark streets tossing news-papers on porches. And if he had wanted another job, what chance was there? Grown men were being thrown out of work all over the place. Martin's own father had lost his job three years ago, and after four horrible months got another, not as good. Not any way as good. Berry Madden's old man had lost his and hadn't got another yet, in over a year. The entire Madden bunch had had to move in with Mrs. Madden's parents.

How would you like that? Martin asked himself. He and Marietta had two sets of grandparents. His father's people, who lived in Arizona, had only been east twice in Martin's lifetime. They were good about Christmas and birthdays. He and his sister knew their mother's parents much better. They'd only left Missouri a few years ago, for Grandma's health, tak-ing their furniture and their nippy-yippy dog, Pep-per, with them. Martin liked them all well enough but could go months without thinking of them. One thing sure—he would *not* want to crowd in with either set.

He tried to find comfort in Berry's misfortune, but somehow that never did seem to work—counting up how many people were worse off than you were. Things were tough for Berry, but that was his problem. Martin had his own. There was nothing *welcoming* in his life. Not anywhere.

There was no warm furry being with brown eyes full of love that said, I've been waiting all day to see you.

"Ah, Rufe," he murmured shakily. "Rufus, I sure do miss you." Five years was a long long time to wait.

He sat on his mattress, leaning forward, waiting until the dangerous need to cry had passed.

After a long while, with an effort, he shrugged. It was the most satisfying gesture he knew. It said everything without a word. It said, The heck with all of you and who cares anyway, not me, so bug off, the bunch of you. Including you, Rufe.

Having got all this across with a movement of his shoulders, he picked up *Quest for a Continent,* by Walter Sullivan, and presently was lost in the Antarctic wastes, with men who struggled on, with no help from the outside world, in the howling winds, the sleety snow, the vast and icy aloneness of a world they'd come to conquer that had finally conquered them.

3

"Martin! Martin Hastings!" Marietta called up the stairs. "I'm going to eat. Do you want to eat with me or wait for them?"

Martin emerged from the Bay of Whales, where he'd been guiding the icebreaker *Northwind* through a path imperiled by calving icebergs.

"What time is it?" he yelled down.

"Six-thirty, and it doesn't make any difference what time it is. I'm hungry now. Are you coming down or aren't you?"

"Sure, sure."

In the kitchen, Marietta was already dishing up stew on two plates. "You want a roll, too, I suppose? There are potatoes in the stew."

"I still want a roll."

"A person should not eat more than one starch at a meal."

"I'm starved. I've been man-hauling my sledge—"

"Oh, Marty, can it, will you? You're getting to be a bore. If you want to read all that stuff, fine, but stop with the dreams of glory, okay?"

Martin flushed. He was like his father, easily snubbed. "I was just pretending," he muttered.

"Well, I know *that*. I didn't think you were really—oh, for goodness sakes, sit. I didn't mean to hurt your little feelings. For somebody who weighs what you do, you certainly have a thin skin."

Martin started out of the kitchen.

"Marty! Come back! I'm sorry, I take it back. I take everything back, absolutely everything! I spun dried your sleeping bag. It's hanging in the cellar. You'll have to use sheets and blankets tonight. Now come on, Martin. Come and eat before it's cold."

Martin sat, tried to poke at his food as if without appetite, and failed. How had they got *along* on a slice of pemmican and a pannikin of tea?

"Thanks," he said with his mouth full. "Why're you in such a rush?"

"I'm baby-sitting at Weavers' down the street. That pest, Ryan. I have to be there by seven."

"What do they pay you?"

"That is none of your business."

"I bet I could do that. No reason why a boy couldn't baby-sit. Probably if it was for boys, they'd like it a

23

lot better than some girl doing it. I could baby-sit boys. You take the girl jobs and I'll—"

Marietta got up, took her plate and glass to the sink. "There's Jell-O and cookies for dessert. I don't have time. Put the dishes in the washer when you're finished."

"Marietta, I was *saying* something."

"And I wasn't listening. You don't know the first thing about— Look, I feed the children, and bathe them, and play games, and read to them and put them to bed. You couldn't do that. Besides, there isn't a mother on this block would let you anywhere near her kids, and if you don't know that—"

"I am not—like I used to be," he said to his sister with dignity. "I don't—I'm not like that anymore, and you know it."

"Maybe. Well, let's hope your new self gets revealed to the public before you're thirty years old."

Martin looked at her bleakly. "Why do you suppose nobody in this house is ever really nice to anybody?"

Marietta turned her hands out, with a little sigh. "How should I know, Marty? Mama's too rushed and tired. Dad—he seems to have this—this sort of *grudge* all the time."

"At what?"

"Who knows? Maybe he's going to lose his job

again. I don't think that Mr. Gaylord likes him very much."

"Don't *say* that!"

"You asked," Marietta said. "Look, I have to get going."

"Why do you want to be eighteen and away from us all? I mean, I want to be, too," he said, betting with himself that she wouldn't ask why. She didn't.

"Oh, my goodness, Martin," she said, "will you stop nagging. I don't know that, I don't know this, I don't know *why*. I just get tired of the way we are. I know girls—in their house the telephone rings, and people come for dinner, and they have *friends* and get a lot of Christmas cards. How many friends do we have?"

"You have nice ones," he said thoughtfully. "You get to stay overnight in people's houses, and girls telephone you." He was about to add, "And you telephone boys," but held his tongue.

"I suppose I do. Yes, all right. I have some nice friends. But what I meant—our family seems so *out* of things."

After she'd gone, Martin sat at the table brooding. Didn't Mr. Gaylord like his father? Mr. Gaylord was not only the boss, he was the man who'd given Rufus to Martin and then taken him back when Martin turned out not to be responsible. Martin didn't even like the sound of his name. What would happen about him and Rufe if his father lost this job, too?

He sighed as he rinsed the few plates and put them in the dishwasher. Then he got his books and settled at the table to do homework.

Just the same, he thought, staring at his algebra book, Marietta hadn't always had friends, or been sure of herself, the way she seemed now. Martin could recall, not more than a couple of years ago, when she'd been invited to her first boy-girl party and had refused to go. When Mrs. Hastings asked why, she'd just cried noisily.

"Who's going to pay any attention to me?" Martin overheard her saying. "What boy will *dance* with me? I'm too tall and I don't have any development and I get so *nervous.*"

"Marietta," their mother said, "you are a lovely-looking girl. Simply lovely. If I were at that party, you'd be the very first girl I'd ask to dance."

"Mother! You aren't going to be at the party, and you are not a boy!"

She'd stayed home and cried some more and then got over it. Now she had friends and went to parties and didn't seem to be nervous about anything.

So maybe there's hope for me, too, Martin thought.

When he heard his father's car turn into the drive-way and the garage door go up, his stomach muscles tensed.

"Hey, I'm sorry about the lights Dad," he said, when Mr. Hastings came in the back door. "I was so busy working on my algebra here that I—"

"Forget it. What's for dinner?"

"Stew. I'll heat it for you right away."

"Give it to me in the living room," said Mr. Hastings, taking off his coat as he walked down the hall.

He was sitting in front of the television, watching the news, when Martin brought the tray in. "Thanks," he said, not looking up.

"Pretty cold today," Martin said, hovering.

"Yup."

"Great weather for penguins."

"What's that?"

"Do you want your coffee now?"

"Later. Marty, I'm trying to listen to this, find out what they're doing to us." But with a sudden snort of disgust, he turned the television off. "The more you find out, the worse you feel. I swear, sometimes I think it'd be better just to ignore the news. Can't do anything about anything anyway." He fixed his eyes on Martin. "Well, how are things?"

"Fine, Dad."

"Everything all right in school? Passing everything, are you?"

"Oh, yes. Yes, I am."

"Good, good."

Maybe this was the time to start a conversation. Have a talk about something, just the two of them.

"How'd *your* day go, Dad?" he asked abruptly. "Anything special happen?"

Mr. Hastings looked startled. "My day? Nothing special ever happens in my day. I do my job."

"Oh, sure Dad. That's for sure, all right. I just thought, you know, you might want to talk about it or something."

"Well, I don't." Mr. Hastings glanced at the blank TV screen, looked back to his son. "No offense, Marty. I just don't have anything to say jobwise."

"That's okay." Martin thought he'd better get back to his homework, but remained where he was. He thought of saying, "Dad, do you ever notice that I don't have many friends?" *Any* friends? Did his father wonder why his son didn't lead the sort of Tom Sawyer life that some boys—*most* boys?—led? Friends around the house, visits to the houses of friends, telephone calls—that sort of thing?

If he did, he never said. What kind of boy's life,

Martin wondered suddenly, had his father had? "What did you do when you were a boy?" he asked.

"Do? I just was a boy, and then I grew up. Like everybody else."

"You don't remember anything—special? About how you were? Or how you felt, maybe?"

"Felt about what?" Mr. Hastings asked. He studied Martin's face. "What's this about? You in trouble of some kind?"

"No, I'm not. No kind at all."

There was always a moment in his father's company when Martin dove for the nearest hole. Now he jumped up saying, "I'll get your coffee, huh? Okay, Dad?"

He was at the door when his father said, "Martin—"

"Yeah?"

"I—just had a regular childhood. Nothing much to remember about it, I guess. I'm sure not keeping any secrets." He rubbed his cheek with his big hand. "You're sure everything's okay with you?"

"I'm sure."

"Good."

After he'd brought the coffee in to his father, who was back at the television and didn't look up, Martin returned to the kitchen, to his algebra. Again, after a moment, he put down his pencil and sat still, think-

30

ing. Maybe his Dad had had a childhood kind of like his own. Sort of lonely. Nothing really wrong. Couple of years of being a bully, of having teachers complain and neighbors storm the doors with lists of his wrongdoings. He'd say this for his father, he'd always taken Martin's side against everybody. Not all fathers would do that.

If I were my own father, talking to a boy like me that was my son that nothing much was wrong with even if nothing much was right, I wouldn't want to talk about myself as a boy either.

Confused by his own syntax, he bent over his work again.

———————

He was still at it when his mother came in, having walked four blocks from the bus. She stopped to hang up her coat, then went into the living room but didn't stay long.

"Hello, honey," she said to Martin, who was re-heating stew for the third time. She shook her head. "I wonder why you and Marietta can't learn that if you just warm up enough for the servings you're— Oh well, it doesn't matter. I don't think I can eat anyway."

"You have to eat, Mom. Keep your strength up. I mean, you work too hard, and riding that bus—"

31

"Later, Marty. Later. Just let me be quiet for a few minutes."

"Sure. Okay."

Mrs. Hastings ate a small amount, leaned back, closed her eyes briefly, opened them, and smiled at her son. "Better now. Where's Marietta?"

"Baby-sitting for the Weavers."

"Oh, yes. She told me this morning."

"Mom, I don't think you should get this tired," he said anxiously. "You might get sick or something."

"No, I'm fine. Today wasn't the best day I've ever had. Some woman accused me of overcharging her."

Martin felt a rush of rage. "I hope you told *her* off. Boy, if I could get my hands on her—"

"Marty! Actually, I had. I made a mistake. But she said I did it deliberately, as if there was some way I could steal her darn money."

"Yeah, but what did you do? You don't have to take that kind of thing!"

"No? Well, Mr. Karl came over when he heard her carrying on, and checked the sales slip and the register and corrected everything and apologized to her."

"How about somebody apologizing to you?"

"Why? I was the one who made the mistake. I shouldn't have told you. I ought to know better. I just thought if I said it to somebody, this sort of . . .

of slightly sick feeling it gave me would go away. But you always overreact so."

Martin looked at her miserably. He'd wanted to help. How could he react except to get angry in her defense? "I was trying to help," he mumbled.

Mrs. Hastings reached across the table, took his hand for a moment. "I know you were, Marty. Forgive me. Try to understand. I know I get short with you. I don't want to, I don't mean to. It's just—" She shook her head and patted his hand again.

"Yeah," said her son.

———

Later, Mr. and Mrs. Hastings sat together in the living room, watching a movie. Martin, carrying his books, glanced in. An old black and white flick. The kind, he thought, they used to see when they were alive. When they were *young*, he corrected himself, partly horrified and partly wanting to laugh.

There was just the one television set in their house, and he sure didn't want to watch what they were watching. He went upstairs. In his room he picked up *Quest for a Continent*, but it was a while before he could get into it.

("Martin, you're getting to be a *bore*. Stop with the fairy tales!")

After a while it was all right. He was reading the chapter "First Air Base in Antarctica," and Admiral

Byrd, his hero, was in the plane as it headed into the wind and built up speed. Admiral Byrd was not at the controls. Still sick from his months at Advance Base, he had given command to Commander William M. Hawkes. . . .

———

Marietta came home at about ten o'clock, called good night as she passed Martin's room, went into her own, and closed the door. Shortly after that his parents came up.

" 'Night, Marty," said his father, not stopping in the hall.

" 'Night, Dad. Pleasant dreams."

Mrs. Hastings looked in. "Where's your sleeping bag, Marty?"

"Crums. I forgot. I washed it," he said, with a touch of satisfaction. "Marietta says it's too cheap to put in the dryer, so I—I mean, she—hung it in the cellar."

"Marietta talks too much. Well, you aren't planning to sleep on a bare mattress, are you?"

"I don't mind."

"Get some sheets and blankets and make up your bed properly! Please. We aren't living in a cave."

"At Advance Base, Admiral Byrd—"

"Martin!" It was nearly a shriek. "Stop that and do as I say. Please! Good night."

" 'Night, Mom. Pleasant dreams."

Getting supplies from the hall closet, Martin saw
that his parents had closed their door, too, as usual.
He was the only one in the family who left his door
open at night. That meant he couldn't open the window, on account of letting the heat escape, but he
couldn't help it. He'd never, since he'd been a little
boy, been able to go to sleep with his door shut.
Open, he had this feeling of still being near other
people, not shut away.

When he'd had Rufus, just for that short happy
time—the happiest time in his life—he'd closed his
door at night, because his mother had actually allowed Rufus to sleep in his room, provided he stayed
on the floor.

Then, of course, Martin hadn't needed people.

He picked up *Quest for a Continent*, let it fall
to the floor, and turned out his light. Lying in the
dark, he thought about the days when boys his age
could run away to sea. Probably, even if he'd lived
then, he wouldn't have had the nerve to do it. They
must have been really tough, those boys of past cen-
turies.

He punched his pillow, pushed his face in it, and
whispered, "Beat it, Rufe. Leave me alone, like a
good dog. Such a good dog . . ."

4

His English teacher, Ms. Schneider, had got him started reading about polar expeditions. He'd had an assignment to turn in a book report and hadn't done it, so one day she called him to her room after school to ask why.

"I guess because I didn't read a book," Martin mumbled.

Ms. Schneider toyed with a pen on her desk. "Do you have a reading problem?" she asked after a while. "Is it difficult for you to read, Martin?"

"I don't have dyslexia or any of that stuff that's going around," he said. "I mean, I can read all right. I just don't like to."

He couldn't remember when he had last read a book. Anyway, one he'd liked. *Tom Sawyer* and *Huck Finn*, of course, but for some reason he always kept those to himself, as if he was the only one who'd ever read them. After Rufus had gone, all he'd bothered to read was comics, partly because it annoyed his parents. He rummaged in his memory. "I read *The Black Stallion.*"

She smiled. "Who hasn't? I got six book reviews on it. I don't think I can take another. But you do owe me an assignment, Martin. If you don't want to write a book report, how about a paper on something that interests you?"

"Like what?"

"Martin," she said sharply. "You must have *some* interests. If you *wanted* to write about something, what would it be?"

"Running away. Well, maybe not running, more like *getting* away. Being some place far off, with no people around me." Just a dog.

"Do you think you could write a short paper for me about that?"

"No."

"Why not?"

"I wouldn't know what to say, how to go about it."

"Would you try an experiment for me?"

"I guess."

She wrote on a slip of paper, handed it to him.

"Go to the library and get this book, and read it. Don't worry about the writing part, just yet. Read it. Then come back and talk to me and we'll see where we are."

That evening he took home a copy of Admiral Richard E. Byrd's *Alone,* and after dinner, when he'd done the dishes, instead of sitting in the living room with his father, looking at a rerun of "M*A*S*H" that they'd already seen about fifty times, he went to his room and opened the book. *Bolling Advance Weather Base, which I manned alone during the Antarctic winter night of 1934, was planted in the dark immensity of the Ross Ice Barrier, on a line between Little America and the South Pole. . . .*

He read that, and settled deeper into his chair.

For the next month he did not so much read Admiral Byrd's book—he was scarcely conscious of reading—he lived it. Walking to school, going through the school day, once in a while playing touch football with the other guys, walking home, eating, choring, his mind was rarely on his own self, his own activities.

He was with Admiral Byrd in that shack sunk in the snow at Advance Base, latitude 80°08′, where the temperatures plunged into the minus fifties and sixties and seventies and even into the minus hundreds. The gales blew and snow swept across the barrier and there was nothing different to see in any direction, only miles and miles of sastrugi—

wind-driven ridges of snow hardened to ice. He lived in the unending dark of the polar night, and on the floor of his shack stalagmites formed, and ice crept up the walls, and the lantern failed, the radio failed, and the undetectable fumes of carbon monoxide from the stove made the admiral sick almost to insanity, and nearly made Martin sick, too.

"Marty, are you all right?" his mother asked one morning at breakfast. "You've been acting peculiar."

"It's all this hardship, Mom. I've been living for weeks on a daily slice of pemmican and a pannikin of tea. Last night in my room the inside thermograph registered minus fifty-two degrees and the ice is starting across the ceiling. The cold and the dark are breaking my bones and my brain and the end cannot be far. I'll try to leave you a message." All the polar explorers, north and south, had left messages for their people to find, before they faced into the wind to die. Search parties looking for their bodies found the messages. Also journals and diaries, of course. Martin knew anything like that would be beyond him, but he could handle a message. He'd already composed several, assuring his family that he had gladly perished in the cause of pushing the boundaries of human knowledge a little further. . . .

This sort of heavenly hot air quite warmed him,

insulated him from the real world. For a while.

That morning his father had leaned over and put a finger on Martin's abdomen. "Doesn't look to me like a pemmican and tea diet. Not with that belly."

Martin's eyes widened with pained embarrassment. His father, not seeming to notice, went on in a friendly way. "So you're still reading that stuff, are you? Good. Reading never hurt anybody."

Other things hurt people, Martin thought miserably. Mean personal remarks hurt people.

His mother, with a distressed look at her husband, said, "Tell me, Marty, what exactly is pemmican?"

He made an effort to respond. "Dried pressed meat with fruit stuck in, like currants or raisins. Easy to carry." Pushing back his chair, he said, "Ah, who cares? I gotta get my books together."

———

Still, he went on reading. Robert Falcon Scott. Sir John Franklin. Peary, Parry, Amundsen, Sir Ernest Shackleton. *There* were heroes. Men to follow to the ends of the world.

A couple of weeks later, he left Ms. Schneider a three-page book review. He'd added a note. "I'm reading a lot of those books, like about Ad. Byrd & some others, their swell. Thanx. Martin Kenny Hastings."

When she returned the paper, he found he'd got a B+, the first of his whole school life. Ms. Schneider had written at the end, "This paper is so lively and interesting that you've earned an excellent grade. If you had paid attention to spelling, it would have been an A."

That didn't bother Martin. B+ was, in his book, just great.

5

Winter licked its frozen chops and charged through January, through February. In the beginning of March, the town awoke to a blizzard.

Martin, when he got up, gazed in unbelieving bliss. It had been an abnormally cold winter, with little snow. Grown-ups generally seemed to consider this one up for their side, but everyone under twenty—fifteen, maybe—felt defrauded.

And now here it was!

Snow was piling up outside his window, driving this way and that, so thick that he could scarcely see down to the backyard. Now and then it cleared away a little, and he saw that their yard, and the Frosts', and all those on the next street over were deeply covered. Fences, garbage pails, toolhouse roofs, whitely mounded. Here and there leafless bushes stuck up, and the branches of trees were lined with fluff. It kept coming, whirling upward, lazily drifting down. Not a late snowfall. More than a snowstorm. A blizzard!

Oh, boy, thought Martin. "Oh, boy!" he yelled. He pulled on his thermal underwear, jeans, heavy socks, his big sweater. Boots, jacket, and his knitted hat were in the downstairs closet.

He clumped to the kitchen, hollering with joy. "Hey, everybody! It's snowing!"

His parents were not looking thrilled, but they smiled as he burst in upon them.

"How am I to get to work in this?" said Mr. Hastings. "And if I manage to get there, how will I get home if it keeps up?"

"You should phone the office and tell them you can't," said Mrs. Hastings. She nodded toward the radio, where the announcer had clearly decided that whatever was happening in the rest of the world, what was happening in Missouri was a blizzard.

". . . the Highway Department has issued travel warnings. Do not drive unless it is absolutely necessary . . . predictions for from eight to twelve inches with heavy drifts . . ."

Martin hugged himself and beamed. There were parts of the country, probably, that could handle a storm this size. But not Missouri. Schools had been closed with *two inches* of snowfall. . . .

"Dad, don't go to work," he said. "Come on out and we'll walk."

"Walk where?"

"Not where. It doesn't matter where. Just walk. Just be in it."

"Thanks for the invitation, Marty, but I'm going to try to make it to the office. Mr. Gaylord would be in a bind without me," he said, looking at his wife as if hoping she'd agree with this view of his importance to the firm.

"What if you get stuck?" she asked.

"Then I get stuck. Probably I can make it if I leave right now, and maybe by this evening they'll have the roads clear. It may even stop."

Ah gee, thought Martin. One snowstorm all winter and they want it to stop. I don't care what the rest of them are going to do—I'm getting out of here.

He finished his oatmeal, resisted the urge to ask for more, and got to his feet. "I'm off," he said. "You'll see me when I get here. Or the other way around."

"Why don't you wait a few minutes," his mother asked. "You can walk me to the bus."

"You're going to work?" Martin asked. "Mom, I don't think that's a good idea."

"Just the same. The buses will probably be running. Will you wait?"

"Sure. But why are you going so early?"

"I telephoned Mr. Karl and he said to get in if I can and probably the store will close early."

While she was upstairs getting ready, Martin sat across from his sister. She was daintily sipping coffee, something she'd taken to doing as a sign of maturity.

"I think grown-ups are crazy," he said.

"Do you."

"Yeah. They get to where they could do anything in the world they want, go where they want, be *free*. And what happens? They get married and have a bunch of kids and they might as well be in jail."

"If our parents hadn't got married, you wouldn't be alive. How would you like that?"

"If I wasn't alive, I wouldn't be liking or not liking it."

"But since you *are* alive, how do you like thinking that maybe you wouldn't have been?"

"Be okay with me," Martin said, after a moment's reflection. "I don't want to die, or anything like that—"

"There's something else like that?"

"Well. There's comas. But anyway, you know what I mean."

"For a change, I do. Well, for my part, I wouldn't not be alive for anything."

"You think it's so great, huh?"

"Not all the time. But I'm here, and I can't imagine not being here. I'd hate it."

"But if you weren't—" Martin began, and decided it was hopeless. He could imagine not being alive, never having been born. On the whole, he supposed he was glad that he had been, but if a person didn't *know*—

"Marietta," he said, "didn't they used to have friends? Like people in for dinner, or going somewhere to play bridge? Didn't they used to *do* something once in a while? Or get telephone calls? Crums, we never even get any *mail* except from the Grands. It's like being in solitary confinement."

Marietta put her fingers against her mouth and looked sideways and down. Another of her actressy gestures, but Martin found it kind of sad.

"I guess Daddy's nervous," she said. "And Mama works so hard. I guess they don't have time for friends anymore. Or maybe not enough money."

At least this time she didn't say that Martin's behavior—misbehavior—had driven all their friends away. Even though the days were past when angry neighbors had telephoned or arrived on the front porch to demand what were the Hastingses going to do about their son, it was still true that most of the people on Barkham Street tended to avoid them. Mrs. Frost, who lived right next door, would hardly speak to them. Of course, in Martin's bully days, Edward Frost—because convenient—had been his principal victim. Only nothing would convince Martin that he had not been equally victimized. Teased and tormented by younger boys about his weight and his clumsiness, he'd been *forced* to take action.

"What's Dad supposed to be nervous about?" Martin hated to think that his father was a timid man, an uncertain man. Hated it. "Marietta, I asked you something."

"How should I know? But you can tell he is."

"Well, *I* can't tell it."

"Good for you."

———

Conversations with his sister were rarely occasions for rejoicing and Martin, walking through the softly descending snow beside his mother, put Marietta out of mind.

"Isn't it great?" he said. "Wait a sec, Mom. Stop for a bit, and we'll listen."

There was a sound to falling snow. A kind of soft rustling that enfolded a person. They stood for a

48

while in the whispering whiteness, listening together.

"I guess I'm glad to be alive," he said at length.

His mother squeezed his hand briefly. "That's good, Marty."

"Are you?"

"Of course."

"All the time?"

"Hardly that," she said. "Nobody could be glad all the time."

"Do you think they're going to blow up the world?"

She breathed a deep sigh and started walking. "They seem stupid enough to do anything."

"Who are they?"

"Who? Maybe God knows, Martin. I don't."

"Dad says they're the politicians and the generals."

"He's probably right."

"So you do think they'll blow us up?"

"No. Well . . . it seems impossible that should happen. Maybe they'll work things out somehow."

"I guess," said Martin.

———

After he'd seen his mother off on the bus, which was late and crowded, he walked on aimlessly. He didn't care where he went, just so he was out here where the air was filled with whirling snow and drifts were gently covering the world—or anyway Missouri—and it was so quiet.

He thought about Admiral Peary, doggedly returning again and again to the Arctic Circle, stabbing through bitter cold, through the long darkness, seeing sickness and death among his men, his dogs. Breaking his leg once. Losing *eight* toes from frostbite. They'd cut off his toes up there in a subzero hut. No hospital. No anesthetic. How did those men *survive* the things they survived? Well, lots of them had not, of course. Robert Falcon Scott and his men, dying of starvation and cold eleven miles from a supply depot. Lieutenant Oates, his feet damaged past recovery, going out into the blizzard to die alone. "I'm just going outside, and I may be some time," he said, and went away so that the three men left behind would not be held back by his crippled feet, so they might have a chance to go on. They had not been able to, but that didn't keep Lieutenant Oates from being one of the best and bravest men who ever lived.

And Admiral Peary. Not as admirable an admiral as Admiral Byrd, in Martin's estimation, but a brave man, too. After his toes were off and he got so he could hobble, he made a pair of sort of toe gloves out of tin cans for his feet, so they wouldn't be banged about too much while he trudged and sledged ever northward. How could he have made those things? And did he line them with fur, or wool? How could he walk with only a little toe on each foot? You'd think it was impossible, but Admiral Peary did it. And he'd made it to the North Pole, after six or seven tries and hardships you could read about but couldn't really imagine living through.

Another thing about Admiral Peary—he'd been a boy kind of like Martin. Misbehaving all over the place. In fights with his peers, in dutch with his teachers, in trouble with the neighbors. Admiral Peary's mother, when he was a little kid, had written on a slip of paper, "We mothers never know what path across the wilderness of life our little ones may have to tread." Mrs. Peary had sure booby-trapped her little one's path. Dressing him in bonnets, teaching him needlework, never letting him out of her sight for a day, even when he got to *college.* No wonder he'd had to scrap and battle his way through childhood. No wonder he'd run as far as he could when he grew up. Even Mrs. Peary couldn't build a nest handy to her boy in the approaches to the North Pole.

He walked in any old direction. Now and then someone went past on skis. Once even a man on snowshoes. That looked like fun. There was hardly any traffic. Only an occasional car having a hard time of it. He hoped his father wouldn't get stuck. You read about people stranded in drifts and only discovered when the snow melted. What would it be like, life for Marietta and him and his mother, if something like that happened, if his father wasn't around? Would they have enough money to survive on? Would he and Marietta have to go to the funeral? He didn't think there'd be many people at it, though he'd heard his father say once that the quickest way to call attention to yourself was to die. Probably Mr. and Mrs. Gaylord would come, if they weren't at their farm. He didn't know if they'd drive the seventy or so miles from there just to go to his father's funeral.

It'd be snowing up there now, on that farm. Rufus would be tearing around, leaping and barking. Dogs were crazy about snow.

He found himself in front of Sonbergs', and wondered whether to go up and ring the bell. His father said that people with even a toehold on civilized behavior did not make unexpected visits. "If you're uninvited and unexpected, you're also unwelcome." Still, Martin decided, that probably just applied to grown-ups. How could a boy telephone another boy and say could he please come over? Otto would think he was nuts.

He mounted the snowy steps to the porch.

6

Mrs. Sonberg came to the door and looked at him for a second as if she didn't know who he was.

"Oh, it's you, Martin," she said.

Nice of you to figure it out, Martin thought irritably. He said, "Isn't it a nice day, Mrs. Sonberg?"

"Nice. Well, yes." She even smiled. "From some points of view, it's a nice day."

She didn't say won't you come in, or I'll call Otto. Just stood looking at him, so that Martin was obliged to say, "I was just passing by, and I thought I'd see if Otto wants to come out and walk."

"I'm sorry. You just missed them. Otto and Berry have gone to the zoo with Mr. Sonberg. Several of the keepers live far enough away so that Mr. Sonberg thinks they may not get to work. He took the boys with him in case they can help."

Mr. Sonberg had the best job of any boy's father Martin knew. He was curator of seals and walruses at the zoo. And now he'd taken Otto and Berry with him to *help.*

With a look of anguish, Martin said, "Help with the *animals?* Help with the walruses and the seals?"

All at once, she seemed actually to see him. Her face took on a dismayed expression. "No, no, no. I'm sure they won't be doing that. They'll be—shoveling walks, carrying trash. That sort of thing."

They're going to help feed the walruses and the seals. Probably go right in the enclosures with them, and pat them. Martin *knew* it. If the keepers couldn't get to work, someone would have to feed them, and it was going to be Otto and Berry. Didn't Otto know—didn't he *have* to know—what it would have meant to Martin to go to the zoo with the rest of them and help with the animals?

"I'm really sorry," Mrs. Sonberg said, sounding now as if she meant it.

"It's okay," he said. "Well, I'll be going along. Tell—" He turned and went down the steps, almost stumbling.

"Martin!"

He waved an arm, not looking around, and called, "That's fine, Mrs. Sonberg. I gotta go."

He turned toward home. He wanted to be in his own house, in his own room.

Berry Madden had been at Sonbergs' awfully early in the morning. So probably he'd spent the night there. Jeb McCrae and Otto often spent a night or so at each other's houses, so why not Berry? Personally, Martin had never spent a night at another boy's house. Once he'd asked his mother if he could invite Otto for the weekend, but she'd said, "Martin, you know how your father feels about having his weekends disturbed."

Disturbed, for Admiral Byrd's sake! The only way the Hastings family could be less disturbed was if they were all four laid out in their coffins.

Was his father, even now, stuck in a drift with the snow piling over the car so deep that they'd never find him until the spring thaw? After the first part, freezing to death wasn't so bad. All the explorers said that. It seemed you got numb and then actually sort of dreamy and content as you froze your way out of existence. So, if his father did happen to—

Martin shuddered and shook his head so hard he got a crick in his neck.

On Barkham Street, in his front yard, Edward Frost was trying to make a snowman. Argess, Edward's collie, was lunging about, covered with snow, pushing her nose through it, now and then leaping at Edward, who laughed and shoved her away.

In the old days, Martin would have plodded past, unless Edward made some remark that required his attention. Now he stood looking at the two of them, Edward and his dog, having a good time.

Edward glanced up, studied Martin for a moment, looked at his snowman, and said, "Not so hot, huh?"

"Can't be so hot on a day like this," said Martin. Pretty feeble, but Edward laughed.

Another moment passed, and then Edward said, "You any good at making these?"

"Not so bad," said Martin. It was true. He had a way with snowmen.

"Wanna help?"

"Okay."

Edward was two years younger than Martin and for the first few minutes this was a worry. Suppose some of the guys came by and saw him playing with a kid? The "guys" were Otto and Jeb and Berry. He didn't know where Jeb was and didn't want to think about where Otto and Berry were. Presently, shaping and sculpting, patting and smoothing, *constructing* the snowman, he quit worrying about what anyone would think. He—they—were having a good time.

Argess was a friendly creature. She paid almost as much attention to Martin as to Edward as she did her best to interfere with the work in progress. Martin noticed that Edward didn't seem to mind. When he'd had Rufus he hadn't, really, wanted old Rufe even to look at anyone but him, though he'd pretended otherwise. And, in fact, Rufus had not— well, hardly ever—noticed anyone but Martin. They'd filled each other's hearts and needs.

Argess leaped against him and Martin held her close, ruffling the elegant head. Rufus was a mongrel. Mongrels, of course, were sturdier and smarter than purebreds, which Argess practically was.

"How's Rufus?" Edward asked, not surprisingly.

"Okay. He's on this farm upstate. Mr. Gaylord— that's my father's boss owns the farm—says he's the best sheep dog they ever had."

"Gee. That's something."

Martin nodded modestly.

"You ever see him again?" Edward asked. "I mean, after—"

"No!" Martin stepped back and studied the snowman. "You got some sort of hat or something we could put on this fellow?"

"My mom says I can have her old straw sun hat. Would that be okay?"

"Great. You know, if we could put a tie on him—"

59

He sure wasn't going to borrow anything of his father's, but he didn't want Edward to contribute all the snowman's adornment. "I've got a tie, myself," he said, brightening.

"Hey, Marty. I didn't mean to—you know, get you upset or anything. Asking that about Rufus. I just thought maybe you had—" Edward broke off.

"I'm not upset. Besides, my father says some day when the weather gets better, we'll drive up there to see him."

"Boy, I bet he'll be glad to see you."

"Yeah," Martin said dreamily. "He sure would." He did not think the weather would ever be good enough so that his father would drive all the way to that farm just so Martin and Rufus could see each other.

Presently he went home to get his tie. The house was empty, the thermostat turned way down, as they set it during the day when no one was home. Marietta had left a note on the hall table, as she was supposed to do, telling where she'd gone. Martin didn't read it.

He walked slowly upstairs, thinking how cold and empty his house was. But it didn't, it seemed to him, feel all that different from lots of times when they were all in it. Why was that?

"I don't know," he said aloud. "I don't guess I'll ever know."

———

The snowman, when completed, was wearing Mrs. Frost's sun hat, Martin's tie, and an old barbecue apron of Mr. Frost's that had "The Chuck Stops Here" written on it in faded lettering.

"That's the best snowman I ever *saw*," Edward said. "He's so big!"

"Do it big or don't do it at all, that's my motto."

"I'm going in and ask my mother to take a picture of him with her Polaroid. Wait here!"

Edward dashed into the house, but Argess stayed and rolled in the snow with Martin. He didn't love Argess the way he did Rufus. He supposed it wasn't possible to love a dog that wasn't your own. But she was a swell animal, and Martin buried his face in her fur, pretending, just for a moment—

Mrs. Frost came out with the camera and smiled at Martin nicely, as if she'd forgotten who he was. Who he *had* been. The Bully of Barkham Street, with Edward here his favorite subject.

Could she have forgotten, really? She and his mother still didn't speak when they passed each other on the street. Just nodded coolly, for politeness. But maybe that was some grown-up thing and had

nothing to do with Martin's terrible past. Maybe they just didn't like each other.

"Get on each side of him, you two," she directed. "Put your arms around him. Edward, see if you can get Argess to lie down in front of him."

"Of course I can get her to," Edward said, exchanging a look with Martin. As if a person couldn't get his own dog to do a simple thing like that.

"Good," said Mrs. Frost. "Now everybody smile."

"The snowman, too?" said Martin, which made Edward and him laugh, so that when the picture came sliding out and developed itself, there they were, laughing like heck, arms around the snowman, and Argess, looking interested, at what would have been the snowman's feet if he'd had feet.

"What a really *nice* picture," Mrs. Frost exclaimed. "Just darling. Here, I'll take another, and you can have it for your parents, Martin."

The second one wasn't quite so good, and Mrs. Frost handed Martin the first, which impressed him. There's manners for you, he thought, and said, "Golly, thanks. Well—" a big sigh "—it's been fun. I guess I better go home now. I guess it's lunchtime."

"Did your mother go to work today?" Mrs. Frost asked.

"Yup. I walked her to the bus, and she got a place

on it. She says maybe she'll be home early."

"Then why don't you have lunch with us?"

Martin looked up and met her eyes. "Golly, Mrs. Frost," he said, "that's swell. I mean, thanks a lot, I'd love to."

Later, at home, he studied the snapshot for a long time. It was marvelous. Very clear and happy. Argess and the snowman were beautiful, and Edward looked great. Even I don't look so bad, Martin thought, poring over his figure and face in the snap. Actually, he thought he looked great, too.

Except.

He decided he'd better go back on his diet.

7

On a drizzly day later in March, Martin came in the house as the telephone started ringing. His mother, who had Saturday off but not Sunday, was home and upstairs running the vacuum, so Martin answered.

"Is Marietta there?" a woman's voice asked.

Might've known, thought Martin. "Just a sec," he said to the caller, putting the receiver on the hall table. "Mom!" he shouted. "Hey, is Marietta anywhere around?" No answer. Just the steady, sort of irritable, hum of the vacuum. He climbed the stairs. "Mom, I said is Marietta here? Somebody's calling her."

Mrs. Hastings turned off the vacuum and shook her head. "She's taking a guitar lesson."

"*Guitar* lesson! Since when has she—"

"Later, Marty. I'm busy. Don't you think you'd better tell whoever it is, in case they're still waiting?"

Martin stumped down the stairs, scowling, picked up the receiver, and said, "You still there?"

"Just."

"Yeah. Well, I'm sorry. I had to ask my mother and she's upstairs, vacuuming."

"Is Marietta there or not? I really need to know."

"Not. I mean, she isn't. She's—she's out." He could not bring himself to say the other. Guitar lessons! He couldn't have a saxophone, but Marietta, just like that, was taking guitar lessons!

"Now what am I going to do?" the woman was saying.

"I could give her a message," Martin said, choking. Guitar lessons!

"Do you know when she'll be back?"

"Nope."

"Well, I guess that's that. I'll just have to cancel my appointment. Thank you—"

"Hey, just a minute . . . this's Mrs. Weaver, isn't it?"

"Yes. And you're Martin, of course."

"Right. And you wanted Marietta to baby-sit Ryan, huh?"

"Yes, only I want her right now. I have a dentist

appointment, and I don't want to take Ryan out in this weather. He just got over a cold. I should have called Marietta sooner, but yesterday was so pleasant, I thought I'd be able to take him with me. And now this rain, and he'd have to sit around in the waiting room—"

From what he'd heard, Martin didn't think Ryan would be good at sitting around.

"I could come over," he said.

Silence.

Then Mrs. Weaver said, "Well, Martin—I wouldn't offend for the world, but—" She cleared her throat and stopped speaking. The Weavers lived next door to old Prune Face Eckman, who never missed a chance to smudge Martin's repute, though it had been a year, probably, since Martin had given him a glance in passing.

"Mrs. Weaver," he said, "I don't know why nobody around here has noticed it, but I am—I'm not how I used to be. Always in trouble, I mean. I'm just about never in trouble anymore, if anybody'd take the trouble to look and find out."

"Now, Martin. Actually, I have noticed some improvement in you."

Well, whoopty-do, thought Martin. He said, "My Mom's home, if anything—not that there'd be any-

67

thing, but just in case, she's here, and you're only six houses down the street, and I don't see why—"

"How old are you, Martin?"

"Thirteen. Marietta started baby-sitting, around the neighborhood, when she was thirteen."

"Fourteen, surely. I was the first person to use her, when Ryan was just two. She was fourteen."

"Guess I made a mistake," said Martin. In a pig's eye. Marietta, Miss Priceless-Perfection, told as many lies as her brother did. Only she usually got away with hers. Martin had concluded that it had to do with the way she could look the lie right in the eye. He tended to gaze over people's shoulders.

"Martin, tell me the truth—you've never baby-sat in your life, now have you?"

Poised for a moment with a lie of his own, Martin took a chance on fact. He tried to recall what his sister had said the job entailed. "No, I never have. But I could do it easily, Mrs. Weaver. Really. Just read to him and play games and get his supper and bathe him and put him to bed—"

"Martin!" She was laughing. "It's the middle of the morning, and I'll only be gone a couple of hours. You'd just have to stay with him. A game or a book would be fine."

"Then I can do it?" he said happily.

68

"Well, if your mother's really there—"

For Pete's sake, he thought, I *said* she was, didn't I?

"—and if she says you can, why then—all right, let's give it a try."

Assuring her that he'd be there in two minutes, Martin bounded up the stairs to his mother with the news.

"Baby-sit?" she said. "I shouldn't think a boy—"

"Mom. That's sexist."

She smiled. "It is. Of course it is, and very wrong of me. Well, go along and yes, I'll be here, but I hope to heaven—"

"Nothing'll go wrong. It'll be fine. Oh, boy. I wonder how much Marietta makes." Thinking of his sister, he frowned. "What's this about guitar lessons? Where'd she get a guitar, I'd like to know. You never said anything about getting her a guitar, and I think it's rotten when I—"

"Marty! That Mrs. Zimmerman that she sits for, who's bringing up those two children of hers alone, *she* gave it to Marietta. She had a couple extra left over from when her husband died. He was a music teacher, and now she has his guitar school downtown. She heard Marietta plucking at the strings one day, to amuse the children, and gave her one."

69

"Just gave it to her? A guitar? Do you know what a guitar costs?"

"Yes. Marietta's lucky. She always has been. Mrs. Zimmerman is giving her lessons in exchange for baby-sitting time. Things do seem to fall into her lap, don't they?"

"Yeah," Martin said dully. "They sure do."

"Don't go feeling sorry for yourself, Martin. It's a terrible habit you have. And being envious of other people's luck. What good does it do?"

———

It does no good at all, Martin said to himself, walking down Barkham Street to the Weaver house. Still, he was often envious of other people. Of their looks, their luck, their superior position in life. He even envied some of the guys their parents. Anyway, their fathers.

Mr. Sonberg. Jeb's father, the banker. He didn't know Mr. McCrae very well, but he seemed nice for somebody so rich. Mr. Hastings said that a man only got rich by licking the boots of the man above him and kicking the face of the man below. Maybe. Martin didn't see why somebody couldn't get rich just working hard. He'd told his father, because Jeb had told him, that Mr. McCrae's grandfather had been a barefoot boy from the Ozark hills who strode

70

into St. Louis one day and set about making a for-
tune. "So *he* just worked his way up," Martin said
to his father.

"Depend on it—somebody got screwed while he
was getting his piles of yellow gold."

Martin didn't think he was the only one in the
family that suffered from self-pity. Probably he'd in-
herited it. It had been handed down to him along
with his father's nose and crooked front tooth.

Mrs. Weaver was already in her raincoat when
he arrived. She looked him over critically. "Well, I
hope I'm doing the right thing," she said.

Martin assumed a reliable expression and assured
her that she was. "Where's Ryan?"

"Behind the sofa." She sighed. "He's put out that
it's not to be Marietta." Apparently Ryan did not
know Marietta's opinion of him. "Not that he has
anything against you," Mrs. Weaver went on.

"Don't see how he could have. We haven't even
been introduced. Ha-ha. No, really, Mrs. Weaver. I
like kids. I get along with them fine. You go along.
I'll get him out from behind that sofa, all right."
This seemed to alarm her, so he added, "I'll lure
him out, like. With a story," he added, inspired.

"Oh, you like to tell stories?"

Do I! thought Martin, but decided she might take

71

that wrong, too. "I'll read him one. I see you have books right there on the table. No, you go and get your teeth fixed and don't worry."

"Tooth," she said, still wavering. "A little filling. Well." She walked over to the sofa, leaned across the top of it. "Come on, now, Ryan. Martin's here, and he wants to read to you. Won't that be nice? He can read you some of the *Noisy* books, all about Muffin." Silence from behind the sofa. "This is Marietta's brother, isn't that practically as good?" No sound. "Oh, dear," she said, turning away. "I guess I'll have to cancel after all, Martin. I'm sorry."

Feeling rejected, feeling really *hurt*, by a little kid that didn't know any better, Martin felt his face flush. That always happened when he felt humiliated, which made things worse because then people knew how he was feeling.

"That's okay," he said, swallowing hard. It had been a dumb idea anyway. Baby-sitting, for Captain Cook's sake. He didn't know any other guy who did that, so probably it was just as well that Ryan had—

Ryan's head came up from behind the sofa. "I don't care if you read to me," he said.

Martin glanced at Mrs. Weaver. "Does that mean I can? I mean, I should?"

"It means he'd like it. Ryan hasn't a notion of good

72

manners. We're thinking of devoting the summer to teaching him the basics. Like please and thank you." She took up her umbrella and handbag. "Then it's all set?"

"Sure thing," said Martin, not nearly as confident as he'd been a few minutes ago. Well, there was always his mother. If the kid got out of hand, he'd yell for Mama. Oh boy, he thought. I hope I can stick it out for a couple of hours. There'd be no living with Marietta, if—

Just this once, he thought. Get through it this time, and then don't try such a dumb stunt again.

Mrs. Weaver kissed her son, who'd come right out into the living room, nodded to Martin, and said, "Don't let Greensleeves out."

"Okay. Who's Greensleeves?"

"Parakeet. In there—" She gestured toward the living room and in a moment was gone.

While the sound of her car dwindled away, Martin and Ryan stood eyeing each other.

"Cookies, I think," said Ryan.

"Huh?"

"I want some cookies."

Martin glanced at the clock on the mantel. 10:30 a.m. Marietta, he was pretty sure, had told him that the people left instructions, long lists of do's and

73

don'ts, for their baby-sitters. They left telephone numbers for emergency purposes. Why hadn't Mrs. Weaver done these things for him? Probably, he decided, because she was in a hurry to get to the dentist. Probably because she figured it was just a couple of hours, so what the heck. Probably because she knew Martin's mother was on tap. Well, I'm not going to call and ask if this tyke can have cookies, he thought, and said, "Sure thing. In the kitchen?"

"Not in the bathroom."

Wow. "How old are you, Ryan?"

"Five."

"Five." Don't look me up when you're ten. "Okay, cookies. And then the books?"

Ryan didn't answer. He walked to the kitchen, got a pan of brownies from the sideboard and said, "You pour some milk."

Martin looked at the brownies. Homemade. That inner voice which everyone is supposed to have, but which rarely addressed itself to Martin, now just about shouted. Those brownies were not for morning consumption by Ryan and his sitter. Even if the sitter, who hadn't had anything like a brownie in weeks, found that his mouth was watering.

"Hey, now. Wait," he said. "Cookies—that's one thing. But these're made for a—a purpose. They're

74

probably for your dinner tonight. You can't have them," he said, surprised at his own firmness.

Ryan reached a small hand toward the brownies, his eyes fixed on Martin.

"I said no! Look, haven't you got some store cookies around? Your mother made the brownies, I bet, for a special treat. Probably you're going to have them with ice cream tonight. Come on, Ryan. It's too early for cookies anyway."

Ryan regarded him pensively, then withdrew his hand. "Okay. Let's read."

Martin experienced a true thrill of triumph.

Back in the living room, sitting together on the sofa, Greensleeves mute on his perch as a stuffed bird, he read the *Winter Noisy Book* and then the *Seashore Noisy Book*. Ryan had them all memorized and said the words along with him. He also pointed out each thing in each drawing. In the *Seashore* book, he put a finger on the whale and said, "I had a whale once."

"Followed you home, did he?"

Ryan grinned. "Most people say, 'Oh, a toy whale, Ryan, how nice.' "

"I know about these things."

"Did you ever have a whale?"

"Had a walrus. Not for long, of course."

"What did you feed him?"
"Pizza. What did you feed your whale?"
"Chocolates."
They grinned at each other, and then Martin went

on reading. Later, they put Ryan's electric tracks together. It was a tricky job. When you got one section of tracks firmly snapped together, another section detached itself. Still, working together, they finally had a respectable length of looping track with overhead spans supported by small building blocks. Then they ran the two race cars, one blue and one red, around the course at breakneck speed.

———————

Martin couldn't believe it when he heard the front door open and Mrs. Weaver's voice calling, "Ryan and Martin, where are you?"

Martin, at the door of Ryan's room, said, "Here. We've been having a race. Is your tooth all right?"

"It's fine. How did things go?"

"Fine. I mean, we had a good time, didn't we, Ryan?"

Ryan nodded. "Come on back and play, Marty," he said impatiently.

"I can't, Ryan. I have to get home for lunch." Ryan's lower lip pushed out and it was plain that he was preparing to yell. "Ryan! I'll come see you again, real soon. Okay?"

"How soon?"

"Very. No, I mean it. I will. I want to."

"My goodness," said Mrs. Weaver. "You certainly made a hit."

77

"He's nicer than Marietta," said Ryan. "I like him lots better."

Filled with pleasure, but trying to sound offhand, Martin said, "Ryan's a good kid. We got along just great."

"You know what I miss," Mrs. Weaver said, getting out her wallet. "I miss the word 'children.' All you ever hear now is 'kid.' *Kids*. Whatever happened to 'child' and to 'children,' do you suppose?"

"Gobbled by goats?" Martin said, and gave a snort of self-admiration.

Mrs. Weaver smiled at him. "Maybe. But I think it's too bad. Well, here you are, Martin." She handed him three dollars.

Martin stepped back. "No. No, really, Mrs. Weaver. I don't want it. I had a swell time, and I didn't have anything else to do anyway—"

"Martin. You'll have to work it out with Marietta, but it's obvious that Ryan's happy in your company, so when I need a sitter, I'd be glad to call on you, only not if you refuse payment. This is a business arrangement. Evenings, it's two dollars an hour."

"Gee. Well, thanks. That's swell. See you, Ryan."

"You remember, Marty! You *said*."

"I'll remember."

Walking home, he felt good, really great. Just like that he'd won a little kid's heart. *Child's* heart. And here he was, practically guaranteed a paying job. If Marietta didn't kick up a stink. What with the other jobs she got, not to mention guitars thrown in and lessons, he didn't see how she could begrudge him Ryan. He felt so good he forgot to resent the guitar.

And who knew, maybe the Weavers had a saxophone tucked away in the attic, going to waste . . .

"Can't tell," he said to himself cheerfully, and went into his house whistling.

8

Martin was not a stranger to the attentions of teachers. The sort of attentions that usually, in the past, saw him in the principal's office, trying to explain his side. Ms. Schneider, awarder of his B+, was the only teacher he could recall who had never regarded him with suspicion that he either did or did not overcome. It had depended on all sorts of conditions. The subject being taught, the teacher's personality and his own, the weather. And, for all Martin knew, the stars.

Ms. Schneider had been different, and when she did not appear after the Christmas holidays, he missed her enough to go to the office and inquire. It appeared she'd left teaching to go back to school and earn a graduate degree.

He sighed and forgot her.

One morning toward the end of April, arriving late at school (with an excuse, dentist appointment), he saw her sitting on a bench in the park across from the school buildings. She was reading, but Martin was so pleased to see her that he decided to interrupt.

"Hey, Ms. Schneider," he said. "How're you doing in graduate school?"

She looked up and warmed Martin with a truly welcoming smile. "Well. How are you, Martin? Sit, sit. Tell me about yourself."

He perched on the bench beside her. "Can't stay. I had a dentist app—" He discarded that as a topic. "It was funny, not seeing you come back. People missed you."

"Aren't you nice, Marty. When I've got my M.A., I might be back. Before I quit again and start my foray on a doctorate. I'm a natural student, I suppose."

"Just the opposite of me," Martin said, with no obvious regret. "But I always meant to thank you, I mean *really* thank you, for getting me on those explorer books. I read piles of them."

"Not anymore?"

"No. I mean, baseball's started. My Dad's crazy over baseball. It seems to me we're always either looking at it, or reading about it, or talking about it." Baseball season was the time of the year when Martin and his father had a subject in common. "I mean, I just don't seem to have time to read." He shrugged. One way or another, he always seemed to be excusing or explaining himself. He was tired of it.

"I can see that baseball would take precedence over reading for a while," Ms. Schneider said. "I like it myself, a lot."

"I guess my father cares about it more than anything else in the world. My middle name is Kenny, for Kenny Boyer. You know, the Cardinal third sacker. Dad wanted it to be my first name, but my mom wanted me named after her father."

"Did your father know Kenny Boyer?"

Martin recalled a morning a couple of years ago when his father, at breakfast, had said, "I'm not going to work today. I have to go to Kenny's funeral." He'd been biting his lip, his eyes tearing, as they had since he'd learned of Kenny Boyer's death.

"I do really think you're crazy," Mrs. Hastings had said. "You didn't even know the man."

"I guess I knew him better than most of the people I'm supposed to know just because I've met them. I'm going to his funeral and see him to the cemetery, to his last rest. It's the least I can do."

Mrs. Hastings had said nothing further.

"In a way, he knew him," Martin said now.

When he got to school, it was already time for lunch and he headed for the cafeteria. As usual, he was starving. In a brown bag he carried the lunch he'd prepared for himself that morning. An apple, a carrot, a bologna sandwich on thin-sliced bread with a thin scratch of mayo. In the cafeteria, he'd get a glass of skim milk. By the scale in the drugstore, he'd lost four pounds. The thing was—was it worth it? It hardly showed at all, four lost pounds. And he thought about food nearly all the time. Hot salty crisp French fries. Sandwiches of crusty rolls filled with bacon and tomato and turkey. Chocolate cake. Pies—any kind of pie. He'd find himself running his tongue around the inside of his mouth, just thinking about hot apple pie with cheese. Sometimes he got dizzy, thinking of things he could eat if he didn't have to stay on this stupid diet. Why should he stay on it? Nobody was *forcing* him to—

"Why don't you watch where you're going!" Berry Madden, bumped into, looked furious.

"I didn't see you," Martin said. "What's the big deal?"

"The big deal is you banged into me and I don't like being banged into. That's the big deal."

"Well, whoopty-do. I beg your big old pardon."

"Ah—go roll your yo-yo," Berry said, stamping off.

Martin looked after him, surprised. Seemed like an awful lot of reaction to a bit of bumpage. "He's crazy," he said to Otto Sonberg, who'd strolled up beside him. "You'd think I'd laid him out with a karate chop."

"Berry's got problems," said Otto as they fell in together.

Martin sure knew that. Berry's whole family was still squashed in with his mother's folks, who didn't want their company. And Mr. Madden was still out of a job. Just the same . . .

"His old man got arrested again last night, for drunk driving," Otto said. "It was in that column in the newspaper this morning."

"What column?"

"It's called 'Police Blotter.' It tells what people got caught doing. Stealing cars, or driving them drunk, or holding up stores, or trying to pick up— you know—women."

"They put that in the paper?" Martin said, horrified. "That's awful."

"It sure is. Boy, would I hate that to happen to

my father. Not that it ever would."

"Mine either," Martin said thankfully. He thought that if his dad had been thrown in jail for drunkenness and then everybody read about it in the paper, he'd have to run away and start a new life in Alaska. Or Australia, maybe.

A person didn't even know when he was well off until something like this happened. Again? Otto had said Berry's father had been arrested *again*. Oh, boy.

They entered the din of the cafeteria.

"There's Jeb," Otto said. "We'll go sit with him. I gotta get a tray."

Martin's heart lifted at Otto's offhand inclusion of him, but he stayed casual. "Got my lunch here," he said. No disgrace to that. Plenty of kids carried their own.

Otto joined the cafeteria line while Martin strolled—easygoing as anything—to the table where Jeb was taking spaghetti and meatballs, bread, salad, ice cream, cookies, and milk from his tray.

Briefly, Martin felt a spurt of resentment. How did they eat the way they did, Otto and Jeb, and stay so thin? It just wasn't *fair*.

Jeb looked up and said, "Oh, hi, Marty. Where's Otto?"

"Getting his lunch." Martin put his brown bag

down and extracted his own provisions. "Oh, heck. I forgot to get milk."

"Leave your stuff. I'll guard it." Jeb grinned. "In case a rabbit comes along," he said, looking at the apple and the carrot.

Again that jet of irritation rose in Martin and subsided. "I'm training for the decathlon," he said, walking off.

When they were all together, Martin trying to chew slowly (as his diet book advised) and ignore the odors that wafted around the cafeteria, Otto said, "No kidding, Marty, you got guts. I couldn't go on a diet. I mean, I might just manage to climb *on* one, but I'd fall off the other side right away."

Martin swallowed. Right this minute he thought he'd give a year of his life for a big bag of French fries and a chocolate shake. "It ain't easy," he said glumly.

"Yeah, but you do it," Otto persisted. "Takes guts."

Martin, who had just about decided to chuck the darn diet, changed his mind again. He went regularly up and down on this seesaw and wondered if it was going to be like this for the rest of his life. Well, as the book said, the thing was to take it a day at a time and not look ahead. Any jerk could stay on a diet for one day. And then another day,

and another, and so on. A day at a time till Dooms-
day, he thought. Still, Otto's praise had heartened
him. The book said that was how alcoholics got sober,
just not taking a drink *today.* Or, in his case, French
fries and a chocolate shake. And since it was always
today . . .

He looked around the crowded, noisy room. "Wonder where Berry is?"

Otto shook his head, and Jeb said carelessly, "Poor
guy. Wouldn't be in his shoes—"

Martin would never have admitted it, but sometimes Jeb gave him a pain. Who was there to admit
it to? Not Otto, Jeb's best friend. Not Berry, who
was always included in the things Otto and Jeb did.
If a guy who was only included once in a while said
a thing like that about Jeb McCrae, it would look
like sour grapes. Which probably it was.

Jeb could be awfully nice. He could be fun. But
did he always have to act so darned sure of himself?
Did being rich make a person that way? Or did you
get born—not knowing beans about rich from poor—
that way? He had a feeling that if Jeb suddenly found
himself a poor person he'd still land on his feet, find
his balance, and go right on being the way he was.

He liked Jeb. But the only really kind person he
could think of, of their age, was Otto. Martin had

known Otto to get pretty angry, but somehow you could always rely on him to be fair. To notice other people, how they were feeling.

Was Otto the way he was because his father was the way *he* was? Martin didn't know Jeb's father, but everything he knew about Mr. Sonberg was swell. He always seemed to have time for his kids, and he sure was more fun than Martin's father, who wasn't fun at all. Too nervous, according to Marietta. Certainly he was a man that everything got on his nerves. Noise, people, bills, children, his job. Even baseball, if the Cards were trailing. Martin wondered if this year, when the World Series was over—and it looked like the Cardinals, four and half games up in the East, might be in it, and Martin sure hoped they would be, only with ball clubs you couldn't be sure, a team would win the World Series one year and the next they'd do everything but score—he wondered if, when it was over, his father would sink beneath the surface to lie low like a frog until spring, which was what he usually did.

"I hope the Cards win the pennant this year," he said.

"Man, so do I," said Otto. "Did you see that diving catch Ozzie made last night?"

Jeb and Martin had seen it. Ozzie Smith, the

dazzling Cardinal shortstop, had flung himself through the air practically behind second base to spear a ball that would've been a sure double for Dale Murphy, the Atlanta Braves slugger. It could even have been a triple.

"They go on the way they're going," Otto said, "it's in the bag."

"The Braves are pretty good, though," Martin said. "And the Phillies."

"We'll lick 'em," said Jeb. "My dad's taking us to see the Astros this Saturday. Either of you guys going?"

Otto shook his head, and Martin said, "Not this weekend," as if he often went to Busch Stadium with his father. Mr. Hastings did, toward the end of the season, when the Cards were playing double dips to make up for games postponed earlier in the year, take his son to see a few. Mostly they looked at the games on TV, or listened on radio if nothing was being televised. Cheaper and easier than going into St. Louis. If he couldn't catch the Cardinals, Mr. Hastings would watch or listen to anything else going. Even in the American League.

When they did go to the park, Martin always took his glove, hoping to catch a foul ball. He hadn't had any luck yet, but the day might come. Berry's father

90

had once caught one, and then he'd gone and hung around outside the clubhouse, waiting for the players to come out and sign it. He'd got Ozzie and Lonnie Smith, and Keith Hernandez before the dopes traded him to the Mets, and Ted Simmons, who'd caught Bob Gibson in the great old days. Berry had let everybody look at the ball and even hold it for a couple of minutes. He didn't think any more of it than he did of his right arm.

Martin found himself feeling sorry for Mr. Madden, who maybe couldn't stop drinking, and tried to make it up to Berry in other ways. In a moment of insight, he thought that being a father couldn't be easy, and maybe even Mr. Sonberg wasn't as perfect as he seemed.

9

A couple of nights later, during dinner, the telephone rang, and Marietta, as always, leaped to fling herself at it for fear it would drop into silence after the first ring.

She came back to the kitchen, looking peevish. "For you, Daddy."

Equally annoyed, Mr. Hastings said, "Who *is* it?"

"Mr. Gaylord."

"Oh, for—" He threw his napkin down and marched out. The rest of them chewed in silence until he returned. "How do you like that. He wants me—puts it as a request, mind—to drive to his farm tomorrow with some policies he left at the office." He looked around, his jaw set. "Saturday! If I got up at dawn, I couldn't be back here for game time."

"It's a nice drive," Mrs. Hastings offered in an unhopeful tone. "And the weather's lovely. Why don't you just decide to enjoy something different for a change?"

She and Marietta didn't care for baseball. "A lot of men getting together to spit," Mrs. Hastings described it.

"I do not want to enjoy something different for a change. I want my weekends to myself, to do what I want to do, which tonight, tomorrow, and Sunday is to watch the Cardinals play the Astros. That is what I want to do, and it's *all* I want to do."

"Tell Mr. Gaylord, not us."

"Ah—" He sank to his chair. "It's just not fair. He forgets, so I have to forgo my one pleasure."

"Thanks so much," said his wife.

"Oh, I don't mean— You know what I mean."

Since she did, she nodded.

"Daddy, that's *funny*, what you said. Really cute. *He* forgets and *you* forgo. I think I'll make it up into a little tune." Marietta, coming along famously with her guitar, had decided to be a country music singer, but said her real interest was in composing.

Ordinarily Martin would have assaulted her with some witticism like how she played like a bullfrog full of buckshot and sang like a crow, but now he was gazing across the table at his father, hoping to

93

meet his eyes, hoping that his father would think of it before he had to ask.

Drumming his fingers irritably on the table, Mr. Hastings looked around, encountered Martin's pleading regard, frowned faintly, and said, "You could come along, if you want, Marty. See that dog of yours."

Though he might have expected his heart to leap up, what Martin felt was a tremor of apprehension. It had been so long, he had wanted this so much, and now that the chance was offered him, it seemed too quick, too casual. To see Rufus again was something he should have been preparing for, dreaming about. He should have been getting ready in his imagination for this meeting that meant more to him than anything had ever meant to him before.

The big dog, expertly herding sheep, at first was unaware of the boy who stood at the other side of the meadow, not speaking, not whistling to him, just waiting with the knowledge that when their eyes met, when at last he called his dog's name, their long separation would be at an end. . . .

He shook his head, feeling a sense of loss. The old way of losing himself in these silent dramas was losing its power. In the past, he had drifted away in such fancies without planning. He'd just find himself in the midst of daydreams realer than the world around him. Now he had to try, and when he tried it didn't work.

"You're saying no?" Mr. Hastings asked in a puzzled tone.

"Oh no, Dad. No. I just—" He coughed, cleared his throat, snatched a breath. "I just can't believe . . . I mean, it's been so long, and I—"

"You want to come with me?"

"Oh, yes."

"Then say so."

Martin thought he just had, but he said, "I'd like it awfully."

"Okay then. We'll leave early, but I don't think we can get back in time." He rasped his hand over his evening beard. He didn't shave, weekends. Tomorrow he'll have to, Martin thought. He hoped that not getting to see the game wouldn't make him too annoyed tomorrow. He hoped he wouldn't just hand over the policies and then say they'd better be getting back before the traffic got too heavy, or some such excuse. He hoped, feeling really faint, that he'd have some time to be with his dog.

The telephone rang again, and again Marietta sprinted for the hall, and again came back sizzling. "For you, Marty."

95

"Me?"

"I said you, didn't I?"

"But who—"

"Some boy. How do I know?"

Martin went to the phone, picked it up, and said
in a perplexed tone, "Yeah, this's Martin."

"Hey, Marty," said Otto. "You want to do something tomorrow?"

"Do? Do what?"

"I don't know. Hack around. Just, like, *do* something."

Martin's brain was in a tailspin. How could a person have such rotten luck? Two things offered at the same time and he wanted terribly to do both. A chance to see Rufus. A chance to hack around with Otto. Probably this invite meant that Jeb and Berry were busy doing something else, but on the other hand, there were plenty of fellows that Otto could ask to hack around with him.

Just the same, Rufus came first.

"You drop dead, or something?" Otto asked.

"No way. Hey!" He had an inspiration. Not one he'd spring on his father first, since the answer would be no. His father always said no first, and only sometimes reconsidered. Surely he wouldn't say no once Martin had committed himself? "Hey, Otto, how'd you like to drive to the country with me and my Dad? We're going up to that farm where Rufus is. My dog. And you could come along."

"Okay. Wait'll I ask my folks."

He was gone quite a while, making Martin pretty nervous. Probably—well, no probably about it—*certainly* his father was not going to like this, but Martin was hoping he could bring it off. The Cards were leading the league in the East, they'd just got back from a road trip where they'd swept the Phillies and the Pirates, and they were going to be at Busch Stadium now for seventeen games. There couldn't be a better time to ask a favor.

"Hey, Marty!"

"Yeah? What'd they say?"

"Okay. We won't be getting back too late, will we? That's the only thing."

"Heck, no. We'll have to start awfully early because Dad'll want to be back in time to see at least part of the game."

"Good." No one in St. Louis would ask which game. "So, what time will you pick me up?"

"I—I'll call you back, Otto. I'm not just—not sure about the time."

"Swell. That's nice, Marty, that you're going to see your dog."

Martin nodded, then said, "I'll ask my Dad—I mean, ask him what time. Call you back right away."

He hung up, drew a deep breath to steady himself, and walked back to the kitchen.

10

"Buckle up, Otto," said Mr. Hastings. "You, too, Marty," he told his son, who was in the back seat alone. Theirs was a two-door car, with an uncomfortable rear seat that lacked leg room. When the family drove out together, Marietta and Martin sat there, with Mrs. Hastings in front. As was polite, Otto, the guest, was there now.

It hadn't been so bad, Martin thought now, as they pulled away from Otto's house. After the first few seconds last night, when they'd all thought he was going to blow his stack, his father had lifted his shoulders and said, "All right, Martin. I don't see why not."

So here was Martin, with his best friend—even if the reverse wasn't true—in the car with him, going on a ride. And, at the end of the ride—Rufus. He found himself twisting his hands, breathing quicker than usual, and in a way he wished that this had not happened. He'd got so that days, many days, would go by when Rufus did not enter his thoughts, when he was carefree, as if he had never known the joy of having his dog and the deep, terrible hurt of losing him.

Now he supposed he'd have to start hurting all over again. Nothing could have kept him from making this trip, but somehow he knew he'd have been better off if Mr. Gaylord had remembered to take the policies up to the farm himself.

In the front seat, Mr. Hastings was explaining to Otto about the importance of seat belts. "Martin ever tell you about the time he was thrown against the windshield when Mrs. Hastings thought she saw a mouse on her foot and ran into a tree? No? Well, he didn't have his seat belt on, in spite of being told over and over, and wham, right into the windshield."

"How did a mouse get in the car?" Otto asked.

"It wasn't a mouse." Mr. Hastings laughed, as he always did when telling this story. "It was a piece of steel wool that had somehow got stuck to her shoe only she didn't notice it till she was driving and looked down. Women drivers!"

"My mother's a better driver than my father," said Otto.

So's mine, thought Martin.

"Is that a fact?" said Mr. Hastings, passing four cars and squeezing back into his lane in time. But he continued pretty jovial. The Cardinals had shut out the Astros, turned two double plays, hit three doubles, a triple, and two home runs, and had not committed an error. Martin was grateful to them.

He half listened as his father went over the game for Otto, who had seen it and appeared to enjoy the replay. Usually Martin did, too. Not today. He was nervous, nervous. Kind of dizzy. He kept widening his eyes, as if to focus them.

". . . always been the greatest team, in either league," Mr. Hastings was saying. "What men they had, in the old days! Oh, they're good players now, too, but somehow all that money they get, and the free-agent business, and having *agents* for them-selves . . . they've taken something—something *pure*—out of the game, you know what I mean? In the old days, it really *was* the national sport—" He sighed heavily. "Gibson. Musial. Schoendiendst. You don't find men like that today. Or—"

Martin shut his ears. He just didn't want to hear about Kenny Boyer. Kenny (he was always known as Kenny in the Hastings family) had been a super guy, no question, but Martin did not want to listen to recollections about him today.

He retreated into himself. He projected himself into what it was going to be like, a couple of hours from now. Only, as the miles passed, he was less and less able really to picture this meeting with Rufus. Aware of dampness on his palms and a throbbing pulse, he was more and more sure that he wished this had never happened.

They stopped for gas and a soft drink, drove on. Mr. Hastings told Otto the joke about the catcher and the pitcher and the pitching coach meeting on the mound. "Think this guy's got the stuff?" the coach asked the catcher, patting the pitcher's behind. "Heck, I don't know," said the catcher. "Nothing's got to me yet."

Otto laughed loudly.

———

Then they were there, pulling to a stop in the driveway in front of a large, pretty house, with a garden to one side, a big red barn a little way off, sheep in a far-off meadow, and even a duck pond in the distance.

"Hey, this's nice," said Otto, twisting around to look at Martin. "What a neat place, Marty."

I'm suffocating, Martin thought. I can't breathe.

I'm not going to be able to get out of this car.

"Well, Martin," his father said impatiently. "Move it, will you? We're here." He looked at the house, where Mr. and Mrs. Gaylord were just coming out. "Here we are, Mr. Gaylord," he called. "Right on time. Get out of the *car*," he muttered to his son. "Where are your manners?"

Martin pushed the front seat forward and stumbled out.

"My son, Martin," Mr. Hastings said. "And his friend, Otto. They came along for the ride."

"Marty came to see his dog," Otto said.

Mr. Gaylord looked puzzled.

I can't stand this, Martin thought. This's the worst time I ever remember.

"Well, Martin?" said Mr. Hastings. "Don't you have anything to say?"

Martin cleared his throat, opened his mouth, and pulled in a lot of air. "I—ah—I just thought, Mr. Gaylord—I mean, as long as we're here anyway—I thought maybe I could see my dog." Again that look of incomprehension. What's the matter with the idiot fool? Martin shouted inwardly. Doesn't he understand American words? "My dog, Rufus," he struggled on. "I mean, he *was* my dog, for a little while. Don't you remember?"

Mr. Gaylord snapped his fingers. "Of course. I'm

a dope and I apologize. It was you, wasn't it, that had him for a little while a couple of years back."

"A year and a half. I had him for three weeks."

"Whatever. Trouble is, you mixed me up for a minute. The dog's name is Buck. I didn't know you'd

called him—Rufus, was it? When we brought him up here, one of the hands asked what his name was and I just said, off the top of my head, Buck. Don't know why, except it seemed a good enough name."

Martin stared at him, licked his lips, nodded slowly. "Buck," he said. He took another deep breath. He could not seem to get enough air in his lungs. "Is he around, Mr. Gaylord?"

The boss surveyed his land. "Sure to be somewhere," he said. He put two fingers to his mouth and blew a shrill whistle.

From behind the barn came Rufus. Buck. Not a

puppy anymore. A large shaggy dog who bounded over the intervening space and came to a halt at Mr. Gaylord's feet, looking up with his tongue lolling, wearing that sort of smile that well-kept dogs have.

Martin could feel Otto tensing beside him. Even his father stirred uneasily.

"He looks good," Martin said, swallowing hard. He forced himself to add, "He's grown a lot."

Mr. Gaylord leaned over and roughed up the big head. "He's a good fellow. Well, Hastings, let's go in the house, shall we? I'll look over the papers and you can be on your way."

"For heavens sake, Joe," said Mrs. Gaylord. "Mr. Hastings isn't the UPS man. He and the boys will have coffee and doughnuts with us. Milk for the boys, of course—" The three grown-ups started for the house, and Buck, tail wagging, ran after them.

"*Call* him, Marty," Otto said. "He'll come. He— It's been a long time, after all."

Martin shook his head, stretched his neck, cleared his throat again. "It's okay, Otto. Like you say, it's been a long time." Rufus didn't know him, didn't remember him. There was nothing to do about that.

"Rufus!" Otto shouted. The dog hesitated, turned his head. "*You* call him, Marty. Come *on*. He doesn't know my voice."

"Rufus?" said Martin, and then, since the dog was

106

still looking back, he said in a louder voice, "Rufus! Come here, Rufe old boy!"

After a moment, Buck trotted back agreeably and stood in front of the two boys, looking from one to the other, still smiling and wagging his tail.

———————

Going home, Mr. Hastings and Otto talked baseball again, Mr. Hastings telling of the old days, the old ways.

"You kids missed the best of it," he said, continuing his earlier list of grievances. "When baseball was played in the afternoon, in the sun, on *grass*, by fellows who loved the game. Those were the glory days."

Martin, in the back seat, could feel Otto in the front seat having the same reaction that he did himself. If everything was so wrong now, why did his father bother about the game at all? He had never nerved himself to ask this question. His father was not a man who liked to be questioned.

The talk in front went on and on, Otto turning now and then to try to pull Martin into the discussion.

"Whatcha think, Marty?" Seeing that Martin had not been listening, he added, "Think the National League should go to the designated hitter?"

With an effort, Martin responded. "No. No, I don't

like it. Takes something— It isn't as much fun as—"
He closed his eyes, opened them, struggled on,
"like when once in a while a pitcher gets a hit,
that's—" He looked at Otto imploringly.

Otto came through. He turned back to Mr. Hastings and said, "That's how I feel. I mean, I think
it's more fun, having pitchers hit. What do you say,
Mr. Hastings?"

"It was Charley Finley got that stupid DH rule
in," said Mr. Hastings, "and let me tell you, Otto—"
On and on.

I'll be riding in this car forever, Martin thought.
I'll never be home, safe in my room. Safe to let his
heart break, without anyone knowing. Otto knew.
Without anyone *watching*.

It wasn't just an expression, saying a person's heart
could hurt, get broken. *Broken into bits.* His felt
like it had been hit, over and over, with a hammer.

He wanted to be alone with this pain. The only
way he could even start to cope with it was by himself. If only he hadn't gone to that farm. If he only
hadn't seen his dog again. Then he could have gone
on feeling that he and Rufus had loved each other.
That Rufus, in his dog's way, remembered those
three weeks as Martin, in his boy's way, remembered
them.

He hadn't expected Rufe to *long* for him. Hadn't wanted him to. He'd wanted Rufus to be happy until the five years had passed before they could go off together. Only not forget me! he cried in silence. I didn't need to find out that he doesn't remember me at all. I didn't need to know that.

Except—he had gone, and he did know, and the only thing now was to start getting over it, start to do his own forgetting of Rufus, of the five-year-plan, of everything to do with that dog back there named Buck. Of everything to do with another dog, named Rufus.

He couldn't recall in his whole life ever wanting anything so much as he now wanted to be home in his room, by himself, with the door shut.

". . . relief pitchers," Mr. Hastings was saying. "Don't give me relief pitchers! Middle relief, long relief, short relief! They make me laugh. A man used to go out there and pitch a whole game, unless he got knocked out of the box, of course. I mean, *then* they'd bring on your relief pitch—"

Shut up! Martin shouted, and for a moment thought he'd actually yelled out loud.

"Dad," he said, "could you stop the car somewhere for a minute?"

"You gotta go?" Mr. Hastings asked, and added

anxiously, "You aren't going to be sick, are you?"

"No. Just—I want to walk around for a second, is all."

Mr. Hastings drew up at the verge of the road and Otto got out to let Martin climb out of the back seat. He walked across the grass a short way, waving his hand to assure them he was okay. He stopped, took a few deep breaths, and turned back.

"Thanks," he said, climbing back in past Otto.

"Sure you're all right?" his father asked.

"I'm sure."

He wasn't, but he would be. Given time, he'd be okay.

11

"Look, kids," Mr. Hastings said one evening in May, "I hate to tell you this, but neither of you can go to camp this summer. I can't afford it."

"I am much too old for camp," said Marietta, who had gone the year before. "Besides, there's my guitar. I can't interrupt my lessons. Mrs. Zimmerman says if I work hard I should be ready to be in the recital the music teachers give at Town Hall every year to show off their pupils. I haven't been at it nearly as long as some of the others, but Mrs. Zimmerman says I'm an unusually good pu—"

Martin interrupted this flow of self-praise. "It's all right with me," he said. "I've got other plans anyway, more important than camp."

"Plans?" his mother asked. "What plans are those, Martin?"

"Mrs. Weaver wants me to take care of Ryan, mornings. From nine to twelve. Except weekends. Except when she takes him somewhere, of course."

"When was this decided?"

"Couple of days ago. She says it'll be good to have her mornings free. She takes aerobics. Does them? Anyway. And Ryan likes me."

"He liked me too," Marietta said, but not as if she cared.

"I'm going to get five dollars a day," Martin went on, "and contribute half to the household expenses."

"Oh, Martin, that's sweet," his mother said with a little laugh, and his father leaned over to punch him lightly on the shoulder and say, "It's a nice offer, son, but you keep your money."

Martin smiled at them happily.

———

School closed. On the last day of kindergarten, Ryan went on a "field trip." He began telling Martin about it before he was inside the next morning.

"Yesterday I went on a field trip," he informed Martin, then glanced at his mother. "I did, didn't I?"

"Of course," she said. "Martin believes you."

"Where'd you go, Ryan?"

"To a veteran's clinic."

Martin looked at Mrs. Weaver, who said, "Not quite, Ryan. Veterinarian's clinic."

"That's what I said."

"What did you do there?" Martin asked.

"Looked at all the animals and the operating room and the cages and the worms."

"Worms?"

"Heartworms." Ryan sighed. "They were *very* nice. And now I have to write a note to the doctor to say thank you and draw a picture. Mrs. Sokol says so."

"It would be polite," said his mother. "After the doctor took his time to show all of you all those things."

"He's a she. A lady veteran."

"Veterinarian."

"That's what I said."

"But you don't say *lady* veterinarian," Mrs. Weaver began, then laughed and said to Martin, "Later, I guess. I'll teach him that later."

"What are you going to draw?" Martin asked. "And you don't know how to write. Yet."

"Mrs. Sokol says I can dictate." When reporting on school doings, Ryan always said "I," as if he were

113

the sole member of Mrs. Sokol's class. "I guess I'll draw a worm. That'd be easiest. And a hypodermic needle."

"Hey, that's pretty good, Ryan. I couldn't say hypodermic when I was five, I bet."

"Daddy has lots of those. He sticks them into himself."

Martin glanced at Mrs. Weaver, then thought he should not have.

"Diabetes," she said, closed her eyes for a moment, opened them, and smiled reassuringly. "It's under control, Martin. I—we don't mention it, you know."

"I would never," he said. "I practically never tell anybody anything about anything."

Again she smiled. "A prudent course. But the diabetes. Well, that's a family thing. I guess you're just about family by now."

The words, spoken so casually, gave Martin a heady feeling. He looked at her happily. "Gee, thanks. That's—that's nice."

"Martin!"

"Yeah, Ryan. Okay. Which do you want to do first, dictate or draw the worm and the needle?"

"I guess—" He sighed. Ryan took his time when it came to choices. "Draw, I guess. No, dictate."

"I'll go along to my class now," said Mrs. Weaver. "You know where the paper and pencils and crayons are, Marty. Cold cuts, rye bread, raw carrots for lunch. I made brownies. The kind you can eat."

They smiled at each other. Ryan had told his mother about Martin's defense of the brownies that first morning. "Thanks," Martin said. He wouldn't eat them. He'd been sticking to his diet pretty well this time.

When she'd gone, Martin sat at the kitchen table, pencil at the ready, waiting to take dictation.

Ryan leaned against him, thrust out his lower lip, and gazed upward. "Okay," he said at last. "Put this down. Dear Doctor."

"What's her name?"

"I don't remember. Just put Dear Doctor."

"I've got it. What now?"

"Thank you for the tour."

Martin wrote. "All right. Now what?"

A deeper sigh. "Thank you for letting us look at the animals. Thank you for letting us look in the microscope. Thank you for letting us see the worms. Thank you—"

"You don't have to say thank you at the beginning of every sentence."

"No. Well, that's enough thank yous. Then put— I liked the dogs. I loved the heartworms. I want the cat." He paused. "Is that enough?"

"It's great. A really good note."

Ryan nodded with satisfaction. "I really want that
cat," he said.

"But a cat at a vet's is there to be cured of something. That cat belongs to somebody. You wouldn't
want to take it away from some other little boy."

"Why not? He could get another one."

"You don't just get another pet. A pet is something very special, Ryan. How would you like it if someone took Greensleeves away from you?"

"I wouldn't mind."

Besides being diabetic, Mr. Weaver was allergic to animal dander. Feeling Ryan should have a pet, his parents had bought this bird for him and now they were stuck with it. As Mrs. Weaver said, "We can't give it away, who'd take it? We can't wring its neck. I just hope it's not like a parrot. They live to be eighty or ninety, I think."

Martin had to laugh. "He'll end up with Ryan's grandchildren taking care of him."

But what was Greensleeves' problem?

Martin had never seen the bird move. Not to drink or eat or look in his mirror or edge up and down his bars the way parakeets were supposed to do. He just sat there. Once Martin had gone over to the cage and thrust his finger in and touched the soft breast feathers. Greensleeves had stirred ever so slightly, proving that he was—just about—alive. Maybe he hated his cage so much that he'd lost interest in life? Maybe some instinct told him he was related to wildly colored birds flying wild in Amazon forests? Martin didn't think creatures should be imprisoned. Not Greensleeves here in the Weaver living room. Not Rufe on a run in the Hastingses' fenced backyard. He remembered telling his mother once that no place is big enough if you can't get out. Rufus—Buck—belongs where he is, Martin thought.

This time he almost meant it.

———————

Since that day at Mr. Gaylord's farm, Otto had been including Martin in things a lot. He and Jeb and Berry and a bunch of other guys played afternoon games of sandlot ball. A couple of times a week, or more, Otto—who seemed to call the shots for the rest of them—would phone and ask Martin if he wanted to play. Martin tried his best. He was terrible at softball, as he was terrible at touch football, volleyball, basketball. A disappointment to his father he'd been, along those lines. Along a few other lines, too, of course. But then, Martin didn't see how, short of getting to the major leagues, he could help out in that part of his father's dreams.

Martin was a good swimmer. In spite of his weight, he had always been a good walker. Make do with the talents you have, he told himself.

"Marty!"

Martin blinked and brought his mind back from a long way off to the little boy at his side. "Yeah, Ryan?"

"You aren't paying attention to me."

"Excuse me, Ryan. What would you like to do now?"

"Read *The Hunting of the Snark*."

"Again?"

"Yes," Ryan said comfortably. "I like it."

"I'll read a little bit of it, but then we're going to go outdoors, see?"

12

Grandmother Parrish, Mrs. Hastings' mother, was sick again. She was sick a lot, but this time it appeared to be more serious than usual. When her father called and told her about it, Mrs. Hastings came into the living room looking upset.

"Mother's sick," she said, her voice a bit shrill. "Very sick."

"The doctors holding out any hope for no hope?" said Mr. Hastings, then looked alarmed. "Okay, okay—I didn't mean it."

"You did too mean it. You meant it, and I think you are—Oh, I don't even want to say what I think you are!"

Mr. Hastings grabbed her arm and held it while she tried to pull away. "I'm sorry, honestly. It was an awful thing to say. Just popped out. Anyway, I didn't actually mean it. She'd say the same about me, you have to admit."

"Mother would never say such a thing."

"Not out loud," Mr. Hastings muttered. "No, don't be angry. I truly am sorry. For you, anyway. Do you think you should go there?" he asked reluctantly. Air fares to Florida were not in the Hastings budget.

"I do. I am going. She may *die*."

"She never has before."

This time Mrs. Hastings moved away and stood glaring at her husband, her breathing loud. "My father," she said slowly, "is going to give me the money for the ticket, and even if he couldn't, I would somehow get to my mother's side—"

"You've hurried to her side twice before and nobody paid for the ticket then. I can't afford it, I tell you. I'm practically insane with bills now."

"I'm going to pack. If you want to help, you can call the airline and get me a seat on the next flight to Miami that I can make. If you don't want to, I'll do it myself."

"Oh, I'll do it, I'll do it."

Throughout, Marietta and Martin had kept still. At times like these, they'd found it was the wisest thing that they could do.

———

Mrs. Parrish died.

Mrs. Hastings telephoned in the afternoon, and only Martin was home. She'd talk for a little bit, and then cry, and then blow her nose and start over again.

"Tell your father," she said, "that I didn't call him at the office because I wasn't sure he'd be in." She doesn't want to talk to him yet, Martin thought. With her mother dead and all, she isn't ready to forgive Dad for not getting along with her. Of course, Grandmother Parrish hadn't made a secret of how she felt about her daughter's husband, which was zilch. *Crums*, thought Martin. Grown-ups. "Tell him I'm going to stay after the—the funeral—and help Daddy put his house on the market. Martin?"

"Yeah, Mom?"

"Would it be— How would you like— That is, do you think you and Marietta would mind awfully if my father came to live with us?"

Martin's heart sank. Why did she have to ask *him* a thing like that? What did she expect him to say? No, they'd hate it? Yes, they'd love it? There weren't enough bedrooms in this house for another person to come and live with them. Where would Grandfather Parrish sleep? In the dining room? On the porch? Or, he wondered grimly, in with me?

"Martin?"

"Yeah, Mom. I heard you. I was just wondering—what will Dad say. You know how he doesn't like to be disturbed."

"I know that my father is old and alone and—Marty, how can I leave him down here now, all by himself?"

"I don't know," Martin said miserably. "I mean, *I* can't decide anything." His mother was silent for a long time. "Mom, look . . . I'm awfully sorry about Grandmother. Really."

"But you won't give me an answer."

I'm not *old* enough to give you an answer, he thought angrily. Boy, I could've been *out* when she called. I wish I'd been *out* somewhere.

"I can't say about something you and Dad will decide anyway, can I?"

"All I asked was how you'd feel about it."

Pushed to the wall, Martin said, "It'd be okay with me. I guess you can't leave the poor old guy—" He broke off, rubbing the back of his neck the way his father did when he was too tired to talk.

"Well." His mother sighed. "I guess that's the best you can do. Thank you, Martin. I know this is hard on you, and you're doing your best."

"What'll I tell Dad?"

"Ask him to call me tonight."

"Okay. Mom—I'm sorry," he said again.

In bed that night, dozing restlessly, waking from time to time to lie in the dark and say to himself, softly, aloud, "My grandmother is dead," he knew he wasn't sorry. Not the way he should be. A little sad. Awed. He thought he was *awed*. Death. A terrible word. Death and taxes. The only sure things, people said. Taxes didn't interest him. Neither did death, usually. He didn't try not to think about it. The subject just didn't enter his mind.

It was jamming his brain now.

He turned from side to side, trying to remember nice things about his grandmother, so as to avoid thinking of her lying someplace, right now, *dead*— a picture that kept presenting itself to him.

She had been a nice lady, who sent them funny notes with little checks enclosed and good Christmas presents that they didn't always remember to thank her for. His father's mother said that if they didn't write thank-yous she wouldn't send them presents, so they always did, but Grandmother Parrish thanked them when they did and overlooked it when they didn't. A very nice lady. He supposed Mrs. Weaver would say he shouldn't say "lady." Mrs.

Weaver said it was an outdated term. But he couldn't say his grandmother was a nice *woman*. Especially now that she was dead. It didn't, somehow, sound respectful.

And what about Pepper, if Grandfather Parrish came to live with them? His father hated Pepper. He called her a fur-bearing cockroach—

For a moment or two he slept, then a nervous jerk of his muscles sent him wide awake and staring. He turned on his bed lamp and got to his feet, walked to the window, and stood looking out at the quiet street where all the lights were out in the houses and no traffic went by. "Oh, my gosh," he said aloud. "Oh, gosh."

All at once he was ravenously hungry. His belly felt like a cave that nobody had been in for a thousand years.

Taking his flashlight, he went down the dark stairs to the kitchen, where he turned on the light and flung himself at the refrigerator.

He was at the table with a ham and cheese on rye and a glass of milk when his father came in, whiskery, rumpled, sagging.

"Thought I heard you, Marty. Would you mind making me one of those? Or I can do it myself, if—"

Martin jumped up. "I'd love to. Sit down, Dad. It'll only take a minute. You want milk or coffee?"

"Oh . . . milk, I guess. No, coffee. Cold's fine, just black."

Then they were sitting across from each other, chewing like starved men.

When he'd finished his sandwich and was sipping at his coffee, Mr. Hastings sat for a while, looking at the wall. Right through me, Martin thought. A sailor had described that look. "The long eye," he'd called it. "They stare right at you, but never see you. They have a twelve-foot stare in a ten-foot room." His father often had it.

Martin wanted, now, to go back upstairs, but he squirmed and waited.

After a long time, his father said, "I understand your mother asked you—about having your grandfather come and live with us."

Martin nodded.

"Well, what do you think?"

"I guess we have to, huh? I mean, I guess we can't leave him down there in Florida all by himself?"

Mr. Hastings sucked in a huge breath, let it out slowly. He turned his head slowly from side to side. "No, I don't think we can do that."

Martin looked at his father sideways, his habit when asking something he was not sure he should. "Where would—where's he going to sleep, Dad?"

"We discussed that, your mother and I. If—I mean when—the house down there is sold, there'll be some money, and we figure we could have the side porch enclosed, a bathroom fitted in. We'd be able to afford that, with your grandfather's money from the house."

"I see." Martin debated, then said, "What about until then?"

"Until then?"

"Until the house gets sold and the porch gets fixed?"

"Martin, you know the answer to that. He'll have to sleep in your room. With you. You'll give him your bed, of course, and we'll put in a cot for you. I mean, Marty," said Mr. Hastings, lifting his voice sharply, "is there any other solution?"

"No."

"Are there any cookies?"

"Fig Newtons."

They finished off a box of those. Then, for a while, they just sat. Looking out the window, Martin saw that the dark was less dark. A breeze brushed in, a morning signal. A blackbird whistled, and mocking-birds flew past, singing on the wing.

"It's practically morning," Martin said. "I've never stayed up all night before."

"You'd better go back to bed. There's time for a couple of hours' sleep."

"What about Pepper?"

"*What!*" Mr. Hastings slammed the palm of his

hand down on the table. "Blast! I forgot all about that feeble-minded, flea-ridden beast. What'd you have to bring that up for?"

Martin hunched his shoulders, twisted his hands together. "I'll go upstairs, I guess," he said with an uncertain smile.

His father didn't answer, and he went. He wanted to get in bed and pull the covers over his head and stop thinking. Which was, more or less, what he did. He pulled the covers over his head.

13

The house in Florida was left in the hands of a real estate person, and Grandfather Parrish came home with his daughter to be a part, from now on, of the Hastings household.

At first Marietta, Martin, and Mr. Hastings pretended to be pleased. Their manners were pretty good and they were sorry for the old man. He had been married for forty-six years, which was a long time to be with somebody that now you were never going to see again. Without being asked, they counterfeited a welcome, behaved as if it was a real treat, having one more permanent person in a house with three bedrooms and a porch that would presently be made into a fourth.

It took them a couple of weeks to realize that they did like having him.

Martin remarked on it to his sister. "He always seems to be in a good mood, doesn't he?"

"I noticed. Nice change around here. But it doesn't seem, does it, that he's so awfully sad about Grandmother Parrish?"

"You don't know that. He's probably covering up. People don't like to show their—their *sad* feelings to everybody. He doesn't want to come and cast gloom over everybody."

"A little more gloom around here, who'd notice?"

"It isn't that bad," Martin said uneasily. He didn't like to hear Marietta voice his own thoughts.

She shrugged and examined her hands, holding them up, turning them this way and that. These days, instead of splitting one fingernail with another, a habit she'd had for years, she was giving herself manicures.

"What color do your fingers look through those glasses?" Martin asked grouchily.

"I don't know what you're talking about."

"I'm talking, Sis, about those dopey shades you got on."

Marietta had taken to wearing, sometimes even indoors, huge sunglasses that she could see out of but no one could see into. The lenses shifted colors.

"You look like an enlargement of a bug's face," he said. "Like in the nature films."

"Oh, really."

"Yeah, really. And what's the point of wearing them in the house? You aren't some movie star."

"Sunglasses are a cosmetic adornment."

Martin sputtered.

"*If* you'll excuse me," she said, walking out of the room. Presently he could hear her radio, playing softly, and then the bath water running. No more loud rock for Marietta. Now, if she wasn't practicing on her guitar, she played the drowsiest sort of country music, taking the radio in with her while she took long baths loaded with lilac bath salts that you could smell clear downstairs.

You could hear her singing in there. *Here I am, so wonderful to love . . .*"

"Crums," Martin had said to his grandfather. "Get that, will you. What an ululation!"

"If you try to listen with an unbiased ear," said old Mr. Parrish, "that is to say, an unbrotherly ear— you might think it a pretty voice."

"Huh," said Martin.

When Marietta came downstairs, trailing lilac like a broken bottle, Martin said, "Granddad thinks you have a pretty good voice. Anyway, he says he does."

"That's nice. I'm going to be in the recital and I'll be singing, so I'm glad somebody approves."

"Recital?"

"Martin. I *told* you. Some of the music teachers take a room in Town Hall to have a concert every year, and they have their best pupils—ahem—give a recital. I am going to play my guitar and sing."

"That'll be a treat for all concerned."

"You needn't come at all, brother dear." She didn't seem annoyed. She even smiled at him.

It was easy enough, Martin thought, to figure out. Marietta had finally found a boy she liked a lot who would telephone her before she telephoned him.

In addition to his good disposition, there were a couple of other things about Grandfather Parrish that Martin figured had eased his way into the Hastings household.

First, Pepper had been left in Florida with a neighbor who claimed to like her. Mr. Hastings said he didn't see how it was possible, but count your blessings.

And then, Granddad had a little money to contribute. He would have more when his house was sold. Granddad had "savings." Something, Martin thought, you either had to be rich or old or both to have.

"Do we have savings?" he asked his mother.

"Of course. String, brown paper bags, pennies in case copper turns out to be gold—"

"Mom. I mean in the bank."

"If we have, nobody's told me."

Then—maybe most important—Granddad was a baseball nut. At last Mr. Hastings had found someone who would follow him every step of the way through the whole season. Martin liked baseball. Not as much as his father required, not as much as he pretended to, but he liked it a lot. He could not, for seven months of the year, think that nothing else was going on in the world. He couldn't wish, as his father did, that the Cardinals would win every game they played. All 162 of them.

But Granddad!

He was for the Atlanta Braves, which made for noisy times when the two teams played each other. Settled down with beer and pretzels, hours would go by while the two men encouraged their players, bellowed at the umpires, instructed the managers and coaches.

Mr. Hastings would lean forward, glaring at the Cardinal pitcher on the mound. "Take him out!" he'd yell, pounding his fists on his knees. "Get the pig's patootie outta there before he walks everybody in!" While Granddad, watching the Braves pitcher perform to his satisfaction, would smile and nod. Or, of course, it would go the other way around—Cards leading, Braves struggling.

And Granddad didn't think the old days of baseball were best. Mr. Hastings, arguing long enough to keep face but eager to be convinced, listened as Granddad agreed that Astroturf was a disaster and the DH rule plain stupid, but said that he liked night games, because that made more baseball to look at, and loved watching good relief pitchers, and didn't think the players were overpaid. "Doesn't bother me how much they get," he said. "Ballplayers make people happy. There are a lot of people making a lot of money who don't make anybody happy but themselves. Generals and politicians, for instance. I say hurrah for the ballplayers, and let them make what they can while they can. It's a short enough career for the best of them."

What it came out to was that instead of being an intrusion, Granddad was a . . .

"He's a *boon*," Martin said to his sister. He wondered how they'd got along without him. Even when the porch was ready for Granddad's occupancy, Martin realized that while he was glad to have his room back he hadn't, after all, minded sharing it.

14

There were two swimming pools in town, in the same park, not close together. An enormous one with two diving boards, high and low, and a wave-making apparatus; and a smaller one filled with sulfur water. The second had no boards, and icy water so smelly that practically nobody used it. That was the one Martin liked. He could do twenty or thirty laps with the whole thing to himself.

He had learned to swim years ago, when his father had been able to afford summer camp, with Marietta and Martin alternating years. Even when he'd been fat, he'd been a good swimmer and diver. Being fat was what got him started using the sulfur pool. Just about no one around to see how he bellied over his trunks. Now, while he didn't suppose anyone would look at him and think *that boy's wasting away*, he wasn't ashamed of himself. He had a way to go, but could see from his chest right down to the ground. There'd been a time when he couldn't see his feet unless he looked in a mirror, a time when he'd had to sit down to tie his shoelaces, and then came up grunting.

"You know," his sister said one day, "I think it's a good thing you've lost weight. Again. This time, are you going to keep it off?"

Martin pondered. "Don't know. Maybe. Or maybe I won't always think it's so important."

Who could tell what would always be important and what would one day just not matter?

On an afternoon in July, when he was going smoothly up and down the sulfur pool, unthinkingly contented as a fish, there was a tremendous splash and Berry Madden bombed in beside him.

"Wow!" Berry shouted. "Where're the polar bears?"

Martin turned on his back. "Stay in here for a while and that other one feels like chowder."

"Oh boy oh boy. If you say so." Berry churned along, his eyes on Martin, who'd turned around again and was concentrating on doing his absolute best crawl. "Didn't know you could swim so good, Marty."

Martin reached the end, whirled, and shoved back off. Berry stayed with him, splashy but fast.

After half a dozen laps, Berry, breathing hard, said,

"I'm gonna go jump in the chowder. You coming?"
He added, as if Martin might need inducement,
"Otto's over there."

Martin did a surface dive, came up, and said,
"Okay. We can dive."

He wondered if sometime he'd get over this reac-

tion of joy—and surprise—that a casual invitation to take part in what the other guys were doing still gave him. If you'd been outside things just about all your life, did that mean you'd never really feel sure of your place inside? Why had it been easy to picture himself the demon center of Barkham Street; the ace reliever of the Cardinals' first-round draft; the tough, rough wide end of the K.C. Chiefs, when nobody was asking him even to throw baskets in the schoolyard? Now that two or three times a week he played with Berry, Jeb, Otto, and the rest of their gang, he no longer devised dreams in which he received the M.V.P. award and the Heisman Trophy in the same year. He just tried to catch as many grounders and flies as he could before being benched. He wasn't known for his hitting.

There were people who were loners because they seemed to want to be. Others had no choice. Martin was so accustomed to being one of the second kind that he still could not entirely believe he had a choice.

And oh, boy—he'd trade his dreams of glory every time for what he had now, even if it meant spending *all* his time on the bench with guys who couldn't field any better than he did and were so surprised when they got the bat on the ball that sometimes they forgot to run.

139

Funny, how he'd always thought everyone did everything better than he did.

Otto was sitting with Ed Bach, Jim Israel, and Turk Cooper when Berry and Martin joined them.

"You two been in the ice pond?" Otto asked.

"It's really swell," Berry said, shivering. "Gets the old blood flowing."

"I tried it once," Jim said. "Froze mine solid. I couldn't bend over for a week."

They sat in a row at the edge of the pool, dangling their legs, splashing one another.

"That your little brother I saw you with in the park, Marty?" Turk asked.

"No. I baby-sit him. Ryan Weaver."

"Baby-sit?" Turk's jaw dropped. "You're kidding."

"I am not. I get five dollars a morning. Besides, I like him."

"What do you *do* with him, for Pete's sake? I never heard of a guy baby-sitting before."

"So. Now you've heard of it."

"So. What do you do, *baby*-sitting?"

"Read to him, take him for picnics in the park. We feed the ducks."

"Oh, we feed the duckies! Aren't we *cute*?"

"I'll cute you," Martin said, starting to his feet.

140

Turk jumped in the water and came up laughing. "Cool it, Marty. Just kidding."

"Wish I could find a job like that," Berry said. "You know any other kids I could try out for, Marty?"

"But I really want to know about this," Turk said, hauling himself out of the pool. "It's interesting. You take him on picnics and read to him. What else?"

"I'm teaching him to ride a bike without the training wheels. And yesterday," Martin said, warming to the pleasant task of talking about himself, "we had a funeral."

"Who died?" Jim asked.

"Greensleeves. A parakeet. He didn't move around much more before he was dead than afterwards."

A couple of nights before, Greensleeves had toppled to the floor of his cage in a terminal coma. It was the most exciting thing he'd ever done, but Martin wasn't sorry to have missed it. Ryan insisted on a funeral, so he and Martin dug a hole, laid Greensleeves in a cotton-lined kitchen match box, and buried him. Martin recited a couple of verses from *The Hunting of the Snark*, and they decorated the grave with nasturtiums. Ryan had been so entranced with the interment that he didn't remember to be sad.

"Maybe I'll put an ad in the paper," Berry mused.

"Boy available to baby-sit. Boys only. I sure could use five dollars a day just to help a kid bury a bird."

"I get lunch, too," Martin pointed out.

"Speaking of that," said Jim, getting to his feet, "I'm gonna get a hot dog."

There were tables near the refreshment stand, and they sat at one, under an umbrella, eating their hot dogs, drinking Coke. Martin permitted himself a dog, but took only water to drink.

Above the racket—shouts and splashings from the pool, cross-hatching of a hundred transistor radios, high-decibeled conversations—two mockingbirds were singing. For a moment Martin drifted away from the table talk to listen to those joyous variations from the treetops. *That's how I feel,* he thought. Like flying to the top of a tree and singing a million tunes.

"Got a card from Jeb," Otto said.

That caught Martin's attention.

"Where is he?" Jim asked.

"Caribbean somewhere. Scuba diving."

They were silent for a moment, considering this. All were familiar with the glories of the reefs, the eerie and beautiful life forms to be found there. They knew from looking at television. Only Jeb had seen that submarine world with his own eyes. Only Jeb got to propel his own body, goggle-eyed and oary-footed, through its wonders.

Jeb's father was an important St. Louis banker, who gave his son the best of everything. The classiest bikes, cameras, mitts, skates, vacations. In his room Jeb had his own TV; a word processor to do his homework on; a chess computer so that he could play against himself. He had shelves full of books. Jeb was a reader. Jeb was a winner. Jeb was an all-around peach of a fellow, who was always taking trouble to remind people how his great-grandfather had come out of the Ozarks in overalls and bare feet. He was proud of his great-grandfather's mountain poverty and never emphasized, or explained, his rise to riches. Mr. Hastings said that old Mr. McCrae had been one of the scoundrels who got away with it. That didn't explain anything either.

Martin was uncomfortably aware that he shared with his father a kind of bitterness toward people he considered "lucky." That didn't include Otto, the luckiest person Martin knew. He just liked Otto, and could think of nothing that would change his mind about that.

He liked Jeb, too. Who wouldn't? A guy so easygoing and friendly. And modest. Why was it Martin could never shake the notion that it wouldn't surprise Jeb to have people come up on the street and ask for his autograph?

Ideas to keep mum about. He was part of a gang now. He'd never be a leader, never be admired and looked up to the way Otto and Jeb were. They were the long-ball hitters. But Martin was in the lineup now, no longer some lonely dope in the bleachers watching the other guys play. Everybody couldn't be Ozzie Smith. *Or* Kenny Boyer. But two guys didn't make a ball team, either. No way.

Later, biking home, his mind of its own accord started down familiar paths of glory. . . .

Have you heard what that amazing Hastings boy did? Rescued little Ryan Weaver from a fire . . . threw himself in front of an automobile to save the life of a strange dog . . . offered himself as hostage when the bank robbers were going to take an old lady. . . .

A very rich old lady, she'd be. After the police arrived in time to foil the robbers, she'd say, "This boy offered himself in my place and I am going to reward him handsomely." He would give the money to his parents. His mother could quit that dumb job and his father could buy a baseball team. Might as well make it a lot of money. It was his dream, after all. . . .

Suddenly he halted, put one foot on the ground, and leaned over the handlebars, frowning. He was going to put an end to this now. It was time to off daydreaming. Cold turkey. He remembered when his father had quit smoking. Two packs a day for umpteen years. Next day—zip. It had been hard on his father, and oh boy had it been hard on everyone around him. But he'd done it, and Martin admired him for that. A nicotine habit, from all he'd heard, was a terrible thing to break. A daydreaming habit was sneakier in a way, he decided. After all, getting out a cigarette and lighting it and smoking was something you *did*. Daydreams did themselves *to* you. Most of the time he didn't notice he was at it until he was in the middle of the rescue, or receiving the bullet intended for another, or stepping protectively in front of the old lady and saying to the robber, "Take *me*, you creep . . ."

Just the same, he said to himself, pedaling on toward Barkham Street, I'm in the real world now. And that's where I'm going to stay.

———————

"Marty!" Marietta said when he got home. "You have to get *ready*. We're leaving right after dinner."

Leaving for what? Martin wondered and almost asked. Remembering in time, he said, "Sure. The recital. I didn't forget."

145

"Then go take a bath."

"*Bath?* I've been swimming all afternoon."

"Then get dressed. Or don't you want to come? Is that it?"

"Of course I want to." He didn't. But again, why not?

15

Granddad had bought Marietta a lacy white Mexican peasant dress to wear at her recital. Martin didn't see how she had the nerve to perform in public. Once, in the sixth grade, he had stood on a stage, prepared to blow reveille on his bugle (a thing he'd done a hundred times before, smooth as silk) in front of an audience filled with school kids and their parents. He'd made such a mess of it that if the bugle had been a gun he probably would have blown his brains out. He'd persisted, all right, and finally got something sounding remotely like reveille out of the thing. People had applauded him for his sportsmanship, and it had ended up maybe even better than if he'd blown right in the first place.

Just the same. He knew that never again in his life would he present himself before the public gaze as a performer, and he did not see how Marietta could be so *calm*.

For a moment, when she walked out from the wings after the piano player and the clarinetist had done their turns, Martin didn't recognize her. Up there on the lighted stage, she looked different, like somebody he had never seen before. Sort of fluffy, in her Mexican dress. Almost pretty, carrying her guitar, with its new embroidered strap, smiling toward the dark auditorium as if she could see the people. She walked very straight, and in the new dress her development showed more than usual.

She looked like a grown-up. Just about like a grown-up. Martin frowned and glanced at his mother, who had her hand to her mouth and was blinking back tears.

"Crums," Martin muttered aloud. Someone behind him said, "Shhh!"

First she sang a song in Spanish that she'd been memorizing for ages. It sounded nice. The strange words, the resonating voice of the guitar strings, Marietta's high, easygoing soprano—it all came out to something even a brother couldn't yawn at.

When she'd finished the Spanish song, Marietta rested the guitar on her lap while accepting applause and then said in a conversational way, as if she were

talking to a few friends, "Now I am going to sing you a song *I* made up—" Clapping, a few cheers. "This is its first public performance and I'm offering it just for all of *you*—"

She's going *too far*, Martin thought, slumping a little.

Apparently not. More cheers and applause greeted this puffed-up announcement.

"A *zeppelin* of hot air," he growled to his grandfather. The person behind him tapped his shoulder and said, "Young man, you be quiet."

"Ah, stuff it in your ear," Martin said, louder.

Granddad turned and said to the husher, "It's all right, I'll control him. He's my grandson and is just getting over an ululation. It's affected his behavior."

"Oh, dear. I'm sorry," said the person. "I didn't know."

"Of course not," said Granddad, facing forward again and patting Martin's hand.

Martin grinned and gave his attention to dopey Marietta, that stranger up there.

She began sort of—plaintively, Martin decided. A word he'd run across and liked. The guitar and Marietta sounded plaintive.

> *You've forgotten*
> *So I've forgone*
> *The joys that I had counted on.*
> *I thought you'd give me*
> *a little star,*
> *a bottle of scent,*
> *and a Mallowmar.*

I thought you loved me
as I loved you.
And you loved me at noon
but at half-past two
you didn't know me from any-who.

Now her fingers accelerated, strummed and tapped on the vibrant strings.

Ah, my love, my love
You're a real crumb bun.
You stole my heart and away you run.
Sooooo!
To you, my love, my nose and thumb!

Well, as the saying goes, she brought down the house. Even her brother forgot who she was as he joined in the laughter, the applause.

16

On a day in late August, when Martin got in from Weavers', Marietta said, "Your friend Jeb called. He says to call him back."

"What's he want?"

"Now, Marty."

"I just asked."

"Well, I just didn't ask. If a phone call is for you, I assume the message is for you and has nothing to do with me."

"How'd you get that big lump on your forehead?"

"What— Oh, for goodness sakes, Martin. Aren't you ever going to grow up?"

"I need more time, Your Princessness! Gimme a little more time? *Please*!"

"You can take till you're eighty, for all I care."

"Goody. I was planning to start next week, but now I can put it off."

Jeb answered the phone himself.

"Oh, hi there, Marty. Look, the thing is, I don't know if you want to or not, but we're, my parents and me and Otto and Berry, going to my great-great-aunt Nora's for the weekend, to get chores and stuff done before Labor Day, so I was wondering if you want to come along."

He should say he'd have to ask his parents. The heck with it, he told himself excitedly. I'll tell *them*. "I'd like to a lot, Jeb," he said. "That'd be swell."

"Don't you have to ask? Your mother or father?"

Martin closed his eyes. Leave it to Jeb. Leave it to Jeb to do the right thing, every time. Martin sighed and said, "Oh, sure. I have to ask, but they'll say yes. They'll be glad for me." That sounded too anxiously grateful. "I mean, they always like it if I go away." Wrong again. He was not up to more elaborations.

"Good," said Jeb. "You got a sleeping bag?"

"Sure."

"Fishing gear?"

"Yup." He did. Or his father did. A pair of hip boots and a rod and reel, left behind by Grandfather Hastings when he'd gone out to Arizona.

"Okay. So, swimming trunks, a coupla pairs of socks, toothbrush, and shaving gear and you're set."

"I guess I'll let my beard grow," Martin said happily.

Jeb laughed, and said if he didn't hear different, they'd pick Marty up in the camper at seven the next morning.

"What was that all about?" Marietta asked, when he'd hung up.

"I been asked to go for the weekend with the McCraes, and Otto and Berry. Down to the Ozarks."

She surprised him. Sometimes she did. "That's nice, Marty," she said. "I'm glad for you."

––––––––––

They drove south on Route 66, Mr. and Mrs. McCrae in the front of the camper, the boys in back with duffle bags and fishing gear, a lot of boxes and an ice chest full of provisions for old Miss McCrae.

Martin, stunned by the luxury of the camper, was trying to take it in stride. Real chairs that swiveled and were covered with leather or something. A carpet on the floor. Curtains that could be pulled across the windows, but weren't; a table that could be pulled down, but wasn't. A little sink. He'd never seen anything like it in his life before, and was trying to pretend that there was nothing here new to him.

He didn't even want to ask questions about what they were going to do over the weekend at Jeb's great-great-aunt Nora's. It would show that he didn't know anything about what the rest of them knew all about. Even Berry.

Jeb was telling about when they'd first got the camper and had taken it north to Canada. The Hastings family had been to Canada once, but Martin didn't see how to fit in telling about it just now, while Jeb was describing the Badlands of South Dakota they'd gone through on their way north. "You never saw anything like it. I mean, *shapes* out in this deserty landscape like castles or dragons or stuff from *Star Wars*, or I don't know what. Weird. It's all from the earth being pushed around by ice ages and fossils being laid down billions of years ago. Over a hundred miles of it and except for these shapes just empty, and crumbly dry, and hot hot hot."

"What's it there for?" Berry asked.

Jeb frowned. "What a *dumb* question. It's just *there*. It isn't *for* anything."

Berry was unabashed. "Usually places are. They're for storing missiles in or mining stuff out of. Usually places don't just lay there."

"Boy, you really take the cake. What about the Grand Canyon? What about our national parks? Nobody's putting missiles or mines in those."

"My uncle says they're going to be mining in all

155

the national parks. And he says they're storing arms and rockets and missiles all over the place where nobody even knows they're there. He says between here and Kansas City the ground is full of stuff ready to go off the minute the Russians make a move. He says Missouri is going to be the first place the Russians will hit, on account of all that stuff we've got here to protect ourselves with."

There was a puzzled silence, and then Otto said, "What does your uncle know about it? How come he knows so much?"

Berry turned his hands out. "It's secret stuff, but you wait and see. He's in the Air Force."

They were quiet for a while, thinking about possible missiles buried in silos all over Missouri, if Berry's uncle was right.

"Well, anyway," Martin said. "If we got hit, we wouldn't know it, would we?"

Otto bit his lip. "Have you seen those movies, with the bomb clouds going up and up and spreading out like toadstools?"

"Mushrooms," said Jeb.

"Toadstools are worse than mushrooms."

For several miles they didn't speak. Then Berry, with a look of wild delight, yelled, "Hey! Hey, I just had this *fan*tastic idea! You know what—I'm gonna go to a Cards' tryout camp!"

Jeb shook his head pityingly. "You're not old enough, Berry boy."

"I don't mean *now.* I mean, the minute I'm sixteen and until then I'm gonna practice. *And* practice and practice. I guess maybe I won't do anything else until I'm sixteen, except practice."

They were all looking at him, awed by this tremendous concept.

"How do you go about going to a tryout camp?" Otto asked. "What do you *do*?"

"Bring your own glove and spikes and get there early, that's all I know."

"Get where?" said Jeb. "Where is one?"

"I don't know. We can find out. They're all over, in June and July. And my birthday's in May." Berry was bouncing around in his chair with excitement. "How about that, huh? How's that for an idea?"

"What position are you going to try out for?" Otto asked in a tone of wonder.

"Anything in the outfield. I'm scared of the infield. Oh, man. How about it, you guys? Why don't we all go?"

"Gee, yes," said Otto and Jeb together.

Martin was mute. A tryout camp? Him? He wouldn't be let try out for grounds crew.

157

"What'll you be playing, Jeb?" Berry asked, as if they were already running onto the field.

"Pitcher," Jeb said promptly. "A pampered pitcher, or nothing at all. How about you, Otto?"

"Shortstop." Otto looked at Martin. "Okay, Marty. Your turn."

Martin laughed. "Bat boy, maybe?"

"Come on, Marty," Otto said. "Kid along with the rest of us. Nobody's really going to do it."

"What d'ya mean?" Berry shouted. "I am too gonna do it, and nobody'll stop me!"

"Me either," said Jeb, grinning.

"So—what say, Marty?" Otto persisted.

Martin, like Otto, thought that to watch a good shortstop at work was the prettiest thing in baseball. But he had his loyalties. To Kenny. To his father. "Third base."

"Oh, mean *man*," Berry breathed. "I'd be so scared at third base. You really are something, Marty," he said in a tone of such respect that the rest of them laughed till the van echoed.

"Down in back!" Mr. McCrae said over his shoulder. "I can't hear to drive with all that racket."

"Yeah, let's keep it down," said Jeb. He clapped Berry on the back and burst into laughter again, smothered this time.

158

At the first turnoff for Joplin, Mr. McCrae left the highway, and they drove for a long time on paved country roads, turning at length onto a dirt road that went up for a while and then dipped down, curved around.

They were there.

The house was small, weathered into grayish brown. It had a tin roof with a stovepipe sticking out. There were chickens clucking about and a beautiful black and tan and white goat with floppy ears looking thoughtfully over a chicken-wire fence at a vegetable garden that had nasturtiums in a border all around and purple flowers climbing the fence. The goat's kid stood beside her, but as the camper drove in mother and child sprang forward, apparently in greeting.

Martin blinked. This really was a shack. He'd thought when Jeb called it that he was being offhand, as usual, about his family's fine circumstances. This was a poor person's home. Maybe a couple of acres, surrounded by a slab-cut fence with a gate hanging open. They drove through it and pulled up on the dry grass.

Jeb's great-great-aunt was on the porch in a rocker. She got to her feet when she saw them coming, using

a cane. No—a stick, thought Martin. A plain old
straight barkless branch of a tree. Her back was
hooped over almost into a hump. She had a mound
of roaring red hair with a pink flower in it. Her face,

all crisscrossed with wrinkles, had a welcoming smile. Martin liked her on sight.

A young hound who'd been sitting at her feet rose and sauntered down the steps beside her as she made her way toward them. A big striped cat remained on the porch railing, regarding them without interest.

There was a lot of talk and laughing and greetings, and then the old lady said, "Here's someone I haven't met before."

"Oh, goodness, I'm sorry," said Mrs. McCrae. "All this flurry made me forget that you don't know Martin. This is Martin Hastings, Aunt Nora, a friend of Jeb's and the other boys. This is Jeb's great-great-aunt, Martin. We just call her Aunty, to save breath."

Martin put out his hand. "How do you do," he said. He could not call her Aunty. He didn't want to say Miss McCrae, thereby setting himself to one side again. "I'm glad to meet you."

Her hand was so small and light it was like holding a little bunch of leaves. She stood leaning on her stick, but she wasn't trembly and her voice was firm.

"Come along," she said, moving slowly back toward her house. "I've got some Cross Creek gingerbread and cold goat's milk."

"Aunty," Mr. McCrae said sternly, "we ordered

161

you not to put yourself out. We have everything in the camper for the whole weekend's meals, and I hope we'll be lucky and get some bass. But *you* are to do nothing."

"Gingerbread and milk is not putting myself out, dearie. Besides which, I shall put myself out precisely as much as I please. Now, come along."

She mounted the steps, shaking off Mrs. McCrae's offered hand on her elbow.

Mr. McCrae looked after her, shaking his head. "Stubborn. Like a mule. Bring that ice chest in, will you, fellows? Then we'll have gingerbread and milk and look around before we get to work."

Berry and Jeb took the ice chest by its handles and moved forward, but Otto lingered with Martin.

"Not what you expected, is it?" he asked.

"No. I thought it was just Jeb not showing off."

"That's what I thought, the first time they asked me. You know, Aunty is Mr. McCrae's father's father's sister."

"Father's *father's*? She must be *awfully* old."

"Ninety-three," Otto said respectfully.

"She lives here all alone? All winter?"

"The McCraes are always after her to move into town and live with them. She won't. Jeb says nobody can tell her what to do. She does all her own cooking, and keeps chickens and those goats. She used to make quilts to sell, but now she doesn't see so good." Otto sounded as proud as if old Miss McCrae were his own great-great-aunt. "She has neighbors, of course. They're all crazy about her."

"I should think." Martin hesitated, then said, "Her hair is . . . golly."

Otto grinned. "When she was a girl she was a redhead, and she says she sees no reason not to go on being one."

"What a nice lady." Martin sighed, then brightened, thinking of his own grandfather. "What do we do now?"

"Chores. Lots of chores."

17

They worked all afternoon.

Berry and Martin carried in boxes of canned things and staples and stored them tidily in the neat cellar.

Already there was a grand display of glass jars on the shelves. Vegetables, fruit, preserves.

"Isn't that nice?" Martin said. "It's so pretty, all lined up that way."

"She really does do all that herself," said Berry. "It makes me feel ninety-three just to look at."

Otto and Jeb took up the rugs and hung them on the clothesline, where they beat them with fancy rattan beaters.

Mr. McCrae cleaned windows and then the kitchen stove, a big, black wood-burning stove with ornate nickel curlicues for decoration. There was also an electric stove, not very much used. Mrs.

McCrae washed down kitchen shelves and the floor and then went into the living room to clean there.

"Could I do something outdoors?" Martin had asked Mr. McCrae, who said sure thing, have you ever split wood, Marty? Martin had not, so he took a few instructions. Hold the heavy wedge in the left hand, positioned with the grain, tap it in with the sledge, then drive the sledge down hard and there you were, with a split log. Then split the splits and so on and stack them neatly here under the eaves, okay, Marty?

It was more than okay. It was absolutely great. Martin felt like Paul Bunyan as he lifted the sledge above his head, brought it down on the wedge, and watched the logs sever beneath his blows.

After about an hour, he sat on the porch and looked about contentedly. In the uphill meadow, beyond Aunty's fence (he had decided to call her Aunty in his mind until he got able to say it naturally), a white mule was standing quietly, head up, with an air of thinking things over. A couple of crows wheeled and hollered, and a hawk sailed in circles high above the hills.

Bales of hay lay about the meadow, which had recently been mowed by a farmer a couple of miles away, Jeb said. He'd give Miss McCrae enough for her goats and then take the rest for himself. The sweet scent of the cut meadow was still on the air. At the top of it was a stand of pines. Martin thought he could smell them, too, the hot green odor that evergreens get in late summer. He could sniff the fragrance of the raspberry canes, planted beyond the garden and covered with nets to foil berry-loving birds.

"What a swell place," he said to himself.

The young hound, who'd been lying at a distance, got up at the sound of his voice and came over to sit beside him. Her name was Belle, and she was dignified for her age. No scrambling about and crazy barking for this one, with her sad eyes, her modesty.

"Hi, Belle," he said, putting his hand gently on her head. Flat, silky fur lay over the smooth, hard skull. Rufe had shaggy fur, and short, lively ears. Belle's ears were limp and satiny. He lifted one and let it fall over his hand. She looked up at him, then settled down with her paws crossed.

When Rufus had first been taken from him, Martin had found that no matter what he was doing Rufe was always in his mind. When a long time had passed, he could go days without remembering. Until that visit to the farm. That had been like making a new wound over an old one just beginning to heal. Then gradually that ache, too, had lessened. Now he could sit here and feel fond of this nice hound and remember Rufus with love, without pain. He supposed a person couldn't feel any pain forever, without stopping. It would hurt too much.

"Well," he said to her. "This has been very nice, but I'd better get back to work."

————————

"Okay, you fellows," Mr. McCrae said late in the afternoon. "You've done yeoman work, so let's knock off and go down to the lake for a swim."

Martin, by now, was trickling, prickling with sweat, bitten by flies, and his arm muscles were aching. To dive into a lake, to splash about and swim for hours—well, a person couldn't ask for more than that.

Except for Miss McCrae, they all went down the path toward the lake, Mr. and Mrs. McCrae in front.

Martin was deeply impressed by Mr. McCrae. He had always liked Otto's father, a quiet man who seemed to be thinking most of the time. But he hadn't been around Mr. McCrae much at all until today, and he was trying to figure out what it was that made him seem special. Bankers were among the people Mr. Hastings didn't like, but Martin knew nothing about them, and anyway, here in the Ozarks,

that did not seem the important part of Jeb's father. There was something else. He rooted around for the right word, and decided at length that Mr. McCrae looked *durable.* A person who would not go to pieces no matter what happened. In fact, Martin concluded, he looked sort of like Admiral Byrd.

Since leaving home that morning, neither of Martin's parents had entered his mind. Yet now, as he thought about Mr. McCrae, it was as if his father suddenly stood on the path in front of him, hands locked behind his back, wearing a puzzled expression. It was as if he was saying, "But *I* should look like Admiral Byrd to you, Martin . . . not some other boy's father." For a moment, Martin felt truly sad, wishing it could be that way for him and his father, and then the reproachful figure vanished, leaving just a trace behind. And maybe his father wouldn't feel that way at all. Maybe it was just Martin's habit of putting his thoughts into pictures, and then reacting to them, that made him sad. But only for a second. He could not be sad today.

He looked at Mr. and Mrs. McCrae, walking side by side. Now and then they held hands for a bit. Martin glanced at Jeb, to see if he'd noticed, but Jeb was looking back over his shoulder and laughing.

"Look at that," he said. "*Everybody's* coming!"

There came Erica, the goat, and her kid, Tinker, with Belle ambling in the rear.

"We're a parade!" Martin shouted, ignited with high spirits. Everything about this day was making him so happy that he felt like leaping up and down and yelling at the top of his lungs. He contrived to wait until they reached the lake. Jeb, Berry, and Otto raced ahead and cannonballed off a bluff into deep water, and with a mighty yell Martin leaped after them, sank into the cool silty lake water, came to the surface tossing his arms about, gasping with joy.

Mr. McCrae did a jackknife from the bluff, and Mrs. McCrae a swan dive. Erica scampered down the rocks to a little beach, followed by Belle, taking her time. And then they, too, were in the water, with only Tinker popping about and bleating from dry land.

"I didn't know goats swam," Martin shouted to Jeb.

"This is not your ordinary goat," Jeb replied, as they watched Erica dog-paddle about, then leap to land, where she comforted Tinker for a moment before they sprang up the rocks and disappeared in the direction of the house.

"Does she eat tin cans?" Martin asked.

"That's just a dumb idea that nobody knows how it got started. She's *finicky*. Goats are. Like, they only like the best hay. They do eat some peculiar things. They can eat blackberry bushes, thorns and all. Erica likes newspapers. Once in a while she gets in the house and you can't tell what she'll try to gobble then. Aunty chases her out with a broom," Jeb said, and did a surface dive out of sight.

Otto, swimming past, grinned at Martin. "Great, huh?"

"Oh, boy," said Martin.

What he felt, what he had to say, was so tremendous that he could not find words for it. *Oh, boy!* That was the best he could manage.

Otto understood. "Me, too," he said. "Hey, let's dive some more."

———

There was a cookout that night. Barbecued ribs and hot dogs, garden corn, a big salad of garden vegetables, biscuits made by Aunty, and homemade raspberry ice cream that they churned right there on the porch. It was made with goat's milk and tasted marvelous.

Oh, boy! Martin said to himself again.

18

The house consisted of a large room with rough-sawn furniture and a Franklin stove in the center; one bedroom; the bathroom; the kitchen.

Sleeping arrangements would be simple. Mr. and Mrs. McCrae in the camper, Aunty in her room, the boys in their sleeping bags in the living room.

"I thought maybe I'd sleep outdoors, under a blanket of stars," Martin said.

"You'd be sleeping under a blanket of mosquitoes. They come like flights of pterodactyls in the night," said Jeb. "Take my word for it."

Martin decided he would.

Just the same, he wanted to be outside for a while. "I think I'll take a walk," he said, and looked around to see if anyone else found that a good idea.

Jeb, Otto, and Berry shook their heads and yawned. Mr. McCrae was playing cards with his wife. But Aunty got up.

"Good idea," she said. "We'd better take a light. Next to no moon tonight."

"Aunty!" Mr. McCrae protested. "That is *not* a good idea. It's dark. You might stumble. I'll go with him."

Miss McCrae rapped the floor with her stick. "I walk at night under the stars all the time when you aren't here to check on me."

"But—"

"Don't try to *harness* me," she said. "Don't do that, dearie." She turned to Martin. "Come along, then. Just a short walk. Do us good."

With the flashlight making a cone of dim radiance ahead of them, and now and then to the side as she swung it about, Aunty and Martin walked around the garden and started up the meadow. A shadow loped beside them. Belle.

"She's the quietest dog," Martin said. "My dog, Rufus, he's a rumpus maker."

"Belle howls occasionally. A wonderful sound, especially in the night."

"What at?"

"Always when it thunders. I think she bays at the

173

moon, but maybe I think that because she's a hound and they're said to."

They went on.

An owl's call fluttered, and Aunty lifted the flashlight in time to catch a small form drifting by in mothy silence. "Screech owl," she said.

In the meadow a billion insect voices shrilled, stilled as they passed, then resumed behind them. Now and then a pale tremor of heat lightning spread across the sky and vanished.

Once Miss McCrae stopped and gestured toward some bushes. "There's a fox's den over there. I'll show you tomorrow. We'll have to be cautious in our approach. The vixen is there, with two kits."

"Real foxes?" Martin said in amazement.

"Real foxes. Lovely. Animals living in their own place. I like that better than anything else in the world."

At the top of the meadow, before the stand of pines began, was a plateau where the white mule, like a shape of fog, moved slowly, head down as he cropped the shorn grass.

They sat down on a big flat rock, and Martin lifted his head and looked at the sky. It seemed to overflow with stars. Far from any lights, with only a sliver of moon, the Milky Way was a torrent.

"The only other time I ever saw the Milky Way was in camp," he said quietly.

"That's one of the reasons I stay here in what my family calls the back of beyond. I want to see the Milky Way, and hear the sounds of the country night, and know where the fox has her den. I guess I'm just not a person for city lights and sociables."

Martin grinned to himself. He supposed he would never meet anyone who was less a person for city lights and sociables.

"You know," he blurted, "I was born in the wrong century—"

"Oh? What would yours have been?"

"Practically any," Martin said sweepingly. "Up until around 1920." Aunty made a little murmur and he went on, earnestly. "I mean, I should have been an explorer, a discoverer. I *know* that's what I was meant to be. And now there's nothing left to find."

Aunty put her hands behind her on the rock, tipped her head back between her rounded shoulders.

"Do you know," she said, "that Pioneer 10 is now nearly three billion miles away and is still sending messages to us on earth? Whispers of discovery, someone called them. Isn't that wonderful?"

Martin, too, looked up. She was telling him something, all right. Maybe his answer lay up there. *Out* there? He'd never thought of that. The conquest of the Poles had been daring and dangerous and noble. But he hadn't been around in time to help with that, so—

"An astrophysicist, now," Miss McCrae went on thoughtfully. "Think of it. A person with his feet on the ground and his head in interstellar space. You'd call him an explorer, wouldn't you?"

"I never thought about it," Martin said. "I've always been looking backward."

"Well, there you are."

She got to her feet, pleasing Martin by steadying herself with a hand on his shoulder.

"Of course, there's the other great exploration," she said, as they started down the hill.

"What's that?" he asked eagerly. What could there be, besides the earth—now searched and ransacked and found out from pole to pole—and all the endless space beyond it? Earth, and space. That was it, wasn't it?

"The discovery of yourself," Miss McCrae said. "That's the supreme adventure. Every bit as hazardous as rounding Cape Horn, or blasting off from Cape Canaveral. Not a journey everyone dares undertake."

Martin wondered if he knew what she was talking

about, decided that he probably did not, but was left with a suspicion that one day he might try to puzzle it out.

————

Hours later, he was still awake. Lying in the dark, scrunched in his lumpy sleeping bag, hearing the other boys' even breathing, he could not still his thoughts. He went over the day, sorting out moments here, sensations there. He felt again the weight of the sledgehammer as he held it up, then brought it down accurately—most times—on the iron wedge. He restacked the pile of split logs that he would add to tomorrow. He felt again Belle's smooth head beneath his hands, saw Erica tiptoe daintily into the lake and begin to swim. Again he poised on the edge of the bluff, then jackknifed into the deep lake and heard, as he surfaced, Otto's "That was a good one, Marty."

He went over his talk with ancient, amazing Miss McCrae.

He was in a fever of recollection, of realization, of anticipation. Tomorrow they were going to fish for bass and have that for their cookout. Martin had never been fishing. I hope I do it right, he thought. I hope I catch one.

It began to rain. There was a far-off roll of thunder,

and sure enough, out there in the dark Belle lifted her voice in a long, lonely howl. The rattle of raindrops on Aunty's tin roof was hollow and heavy and hypnotic. The long drive, all that exercise, the unaccustomed experience of being with so many people, of talking and listening so much . . .

The day swept over him in a slow, muffling surge.

Dr. Martin Hastings, the renowned astrophysicist, announced today that he has discovered . . .

His lids drooped.

. . . that he has discovered the secret . . . the secret of . . .

He spiraled into dreams, a private galaxy.

About the Author

MARY STOLZ, one of today's most distinguished and versatile writers, is the author of more than 40 books that have been enjoyed by millions of young readers. Among her many honors was the nomination for the 1975 National Book Award for her novel THE EDGE OF NEXT YEAR, and she has had several of her books, including A WONDERFUL, TERRIBLE TIME; A DOG ON BARKHAM STREET; and THE NOONDAY FRIENDS chosen as ALA Notable Children's Books. She is also the recipient of the George G. Stone Center for Children's Books 1982 Recognition of Merit Award honoring the entire body of her work. Her most recent book for Harper is the popular novel CAT WALK.

Born in Boston and educated at the Birch Wathen School and Columbia University in New York City, Mary Stolz now lives with her husband, Dr. Thomas C. Jaleski, on the Gulf Coast of Florida.

About the Artist

EMILY ARNOLD McCULLY holds a B.A. degree from Brown University and an M.A. degree in art history from Columbia University. A writer of adult fiction, she is also the illustrator of over one hundred books for children.

Harper recently published Ms. McCully's wordless picture book PICNIC, which was both an ALA Notable Children's Book and a 1985 Christopher Award winner.

Emily McCully was born in Galesburg, Illinois. She is the mother of two grown children, and divides her time between New York City and the Berkshires.